nsustainable

ns

unsustainable positions

esther selsdon

ABACUS

An *Abacus* Book

First published in Great Britain by Abacus 1994

A CIP catalogue for this book
is available from the British Library.

ISBN 0 349 10550 2

Typeset by M Rules
Printed in Great Britain by
Clays Ltd, St Ives plc

Abacus
A Division of
Little, Brown and Company (UK) Limited
Brettenham House
Lancaster Place
London WC2E 7EN

for annie and les

a moral fool

Nobody wanted to be Cordelia. Everyone realised that you had to do your bit for the group enterprise and each actress recognised that she had a defined part to play in the script and that interaction and pure performance skills were all important aspects of the weekend's schedule but that still didn't affect the fact that nobody wanted to be Cordelia.

The teacher said that the women were being too literal about the text, and perhaps they could just move on to Scene II at this point, since they didn't seem to be getting very far with the religious aspect of things.

Eliza said that she wasn't a religious person. But that didn't mean, by any stretch of the imagination, that she wasn't spiritual or that she had no moral values. Of course not, nodded the other women, confirming their whole-hearted agreement with their philosophical sister. Absolutely. Perhaps we are all just as flies to wanton boys, Eliza added, but I, for one, would like to experience a bit more sheer wantonness.

Cordelia's main problem, it seemed to Eliza, was that she never saw any real full-blooded action. Goneril and Regan were getting laid all over the shop so why did she, Eliza, have to enact the only female character who was as boring as fuck, except that she never did? And then she disappears for three whole acts right in the middle of the play, while Felicity and Madeleine achieved full-throated snogging with the sexiest guy in the cast. And, what's more, they get to lead a whole legion of virulently masculine cohorts into battle. It was a bloody piss-off that she had to be the virgin. She wanted to swap roles, right now, or she would refuse to play with her friends any more.

The teacher said that he wasn't finding this part of the afternoon's study session very fruitful. If none of the other women in the group had any objections, Eliza could play Lear himself for all he cared. He wanted to go home. Women-only groups were always a mistake and he was bound to be late for his tea again just like last Sunday, when his roast had got burnt and his wife had shouted at him and refused to have sex. He wished he were a lorry driver or a man who grades eggs, or anything that didn't involve the multiple, volatile foibles of women with spirit. It was a nightmare.

Felicity told the teacher that she thought he was very perceptive. It was perfectly clear to her that he understood the needs of women a whole lot better than Lear. Perhaps, she suggested as she drew him to one side and blew into his ear, the two of them could go off somewhere quiet later on and explore this area – which was burgeoning with potential – in a little more detail. The teacher scratched his starchy collar. He was writhing with a variety of amorphous sensations and he began to sweat like a pig. This was supposed to be fun. It wasn't; it was a bloody nightmare.

Felicity turned around and, addressing the rest of the group, declared that she hadn't really come to grips with Edmund as a person and perhaps the teacher might like to begin by enlightening them as to a vital piece of his anatomy which was worrying her immensely? I mean, she quizzed the instructor (and he thought it possible that the question might even be sincere), was Edmund absolutely massive or was it just a power thing?

He had had enough. He wished he'd opted for the under-fives group on Tuesday afternoons. He'd asked for something more challenging than 'square window, round door' and now he was well and truly up a creek with no paddle. He collapsed onto a stool at the side of the room and left the girls to row for themselves.

Madeleine had been thinking. She was privately pursuing an obscure section of the text in which Goneril talks about the differences between man and man. Madeleine had a more lyric imagination than her friends, she thought, and suffered powerfully from the notion – which had her husband's full backing – that her critical faculties were in some distinct way more developed than Eliza's or Felicity's. She felt that Goneril was trying to express the idea that it was precisely because Edmund, her lover, was so much more innately masculine than Albany, her husband, that Goneril should be making hay with this apotheosis of desire. It was a piece of unadulterated gender stereotyping, she said to the bemused and uninterested teacher. Why was 'masculine' always so deeply associated with machismo forcefulness? The teacher couldn't tell her and sat blankly, sucking his thumb. Madeleine's husband wasn't 'manly' in this boring, conventional sense, she explained carefully to the group, but he was one of the most fulfillingly masculine men she'd ever met.

'I don't want to state the obvious,' added Madeleine, 'but I also want to add that I think it's crap to call your husband "a moral fool" when you're clearly the one with the morality problem, if you know what I mean.'

The teacher didn't want to be presumptuous but thought that Madeleine was bringing her own agenda to the text. But in the end, he mused, what else was there to bring? If he nipped home now, whilst all the women were discussing the many possible reasons for marital break-up, he could switch on the roast so that by the time Glenda returned with the kids from the football, the tea would be cooked. She'd be really pleased. Then he'd be laughing later. But supposing she was late and it all got burnt? Oh Lord, it was a nightmare.

Felicity was irate at Madeleine's crass insensitivity to Goneril's deeper needs as a woman. Goneril, according to Felicity, is wetting her knickers. She can't believe her luck. All her life she's been locked away in a mediaeval turret with a weedy shrimp of a partner who understands nothing of the subtle complexities of women's sexuality, and then, quite suddenly, she is presented with the God-given chance to achieve a primary source of satisfaction and Edmund's the man to fill up her engine. Edmund and Goneril are birds of a feather; they both have an essential appetite for life and Goneril wants to make up for all the wasted, sterile years she's spent, sleeping, no doubt, on the living-room sofa.

The teacher sighed loudly.

Eliza thought that was an interesting reading of the text but very much wanted to introduce power into the equation. Edmund was a charismatic guy who didn't give a shit about other people and would tread on any man, woman or eunuch who might rashly presume to get in his way. That was precisely why they all went mad over him. He rejected both them and their values mercilessly. That made him an ultimate object of desire.

'He's an outsider and he's rather un-English in every respect,' she continued, 'I'll bet he never has problems in bed.'

'But life is power,' said Felicity, who knew that her reading of the text was the correct one. 'And sex is power. Goneril only desired Edmund in the first place because Regan desired him, too. I'll bet she didn't even fancy him until she realised that her sister did.'

But, as Eliza pointed out, 'fancy' was a very fluid concept, a piece of terminology so vague as to have been rendered utterly devoid of meaning.

'You could say that of all language,' interrupted the teacher, gloomily.

'She's compulsively drawn towards someone who attracts her in a totally irrational manner. It's really fucking her up and she's behaving like a complete fool and embarrassing herself in every way.'

Madeleine pronounced herself shocked at Felicity's negative attitude to one of life's more precious sensations. Love was a wonderful, magical thing and had to be considered one of the possible solutions to the infinite loneliness of an existence without meaning. Its attainment should be treasured and nurtured with care. In the meantime, she added as the other women pulled faces and mumbled a word that sounded suspiciously like 'sentimental', what worried Madeleine was Goneril's global approach to women's issues. You don't have to act like a man to be strong, that's what Madeleine thought. She was particularly upset at Goneril's abuse of the term 'milk-liver'd' as an insult to her husband's virility. There was no question, for the Lear girls, that breast-feeding was a less worthy enterprise than a night down the pub with the lads. They should be ashamed of themselves.

Eliza took a more robust view.

'If you had a husband who came out with phrases like "Proper deformity seems not in the fiend so horrid as in woman", you probably wouldn't feel too hot about him either, would you? The poor kid has the right to over-compensate, doesn't she? Of course, she's a first-generation feminist, but that's because she's forced to be. She'd never get anywhere in life unless she was absolutely committed to aggressive pro-activity. Let's face it, Will himself can hardly be considered reconstructed, after all. I mean, look what happens at the end of the play. It's the men who take charge, isn't it? And it was the women who were the prime movers behind the plot. Edmund would never have got anywhere without the assistance of the two sisters but it's him who gets the final moment of drama on his death-bed and, fuck me, he even gets the opportunity to atone for his sins. It's the same old story. It makes me sick.'

'Ladies,' said the teacher, wiping his brow, and thinking that there was always one in every class but his apparently had three. 'I don't want to cut this discussion short since you're obviously all getting a lot out of imposing your own personal resonances onto the text, but I am the workshop leader today and, as a man, I am beginning to feel just a little bit excluded from the dialogue. Perhaps we could go back to "out vile jelly" at this point, since it just happens to be my favourite scene and I am the one in charge here, after all.'

The ladies told him to shut up. They were paying for the day's instruction and they, therefore, would pick the scene.

buttermere lunchpack

Rebecca and Jerry once met a man in Buttermere who'd never been to London.

They took cheese sandwiches and anoraks and it began to snow. There were no leaves on the trees and the earth was so boggy that every time they stepped forwards they sank up to their calves in the swampy mush. It was no fun at all.

Finally, on the crest of a bleak, watery yellow-green hill, they called a truce and sat down to eat their frozen lunchpacks. The cheese was plastic and the bread was stale.

'I'm having a miserable time' Rebecca said to Jerry, who continued to ignore her.

They had had a row on their arrival at the farmhouse B & B that morning. The farmer was a taciturn man with broad shoulders and a full head of curly, dark hair. He wandered off silently while they were still eating their porridge and so they never had the opportunity that Rebecca, in particular, was relishing – to address him by his first name which, as his wife had told them as they came in through the stunted wooden door, was Ethel. She had informed them quite seriously that the name was a source of great embarrassment to her husband as a child and, having recently had the opportunity to go back to school to study for a psychology A level, she felt herself now in a strong position to conclude that it was this sense of public humiliation as a youngster that had caused him to become such an introverted and retiring adult.

Rebecca and Jerry agreed politely with her assessment of her husband's personality and pointed out that it was a little unfortunate for the farmer that his parents had chosen to label him for life with a name that would have been more appropriate for a girl.

'Oh no, that's not right at all,' his wife corrected the city folk. 'In point of fact, his name is "Ethelred". That's a traditional boy's name. There was an English king in the olden days called "Ethelred the Unready". My husband's parents were very keen on history and when their only son was born prematurely, the name immediately sprang into their minds.'

Rebecca and Jerry looked at each other. Ethelred the Unready? Really? It sounded very unlikely. They went back up to their half-timbered room with no central heating but two narrow, single beds and Rebecca stared out of the leaded window and into the pouring rain.

'We'd better go for our walk now,' she said gloomily. 'That is what we came for, after all.'

'There's no need to sound quite so enthusiastic' Jerry replied. 'You're never going to enjoy yourself if you carry on having the hump like that. You may well be annoyed with me, but the only person you're punishing with your negative attitude is yourself. Do grow up a bit, won't you?'

'I don't know why on earth you think I'm annoyed with you,' Rebecca said. 'Just because you've dragged me up here to a farmhouse that I discovered but that you now claim as your own, and just because the whole trip, in any event, is some sort of sop to your guilty conscience, that doesn't mean that I have to go as far as actually enjoying myself. So don't push your luck, dickhead.'

Jerry shrugged his shoulders. He didn't want to go through the whole sorry tale all over again. There was nothing else to say and he had apologised at least twice. That should have been the end of the matter. He wished she could drop the subject for more than forty-five minutes at a time or the whole weekend would be a wash-out. He looked out of the window and resigned himself to the fact that it already was.

'Which bed do you want tonight?' said Jerry.

'I couldn't give a shit,' replied Rebecca.

'You might be in a better mood later. We might even end up in the same bed, you never know,' said Jerry.

'Fuck off,' replied Rebecca.

Jerry fished his copy of *London Fields* out of the expensively soft leather holdall he had bought the previous summer in a sale in Los Angeles and, waiting for the heavens to close, began to read.

Mrs Ethel knocked but walked straight in. She saw Jerry bent over almost gnome-like on the nicer of the two beds reading a paperback with a gloomy-looking cover. She saw Rebecca staring out of the window with a glazed expression on her face and her hair in a single, solid, implacable plait. Mrs Ethel often saw couples like that at this time of year. She recognised the sullenness and the loaded silence.

She was used to silence, having been married to Ethel for fifteen years, but she knew that these young couples weren't. To them the space between sentences was a burden which they generally filled with sexual intercourse to judge by the antisocial noises emanating from their rooms at night. The cottage echoed with the noises of their love, while Ethel and Mrs Ethel needed no aural evidence of theirs.

Mrs Ethel coughed and said, 'It'll clear up soon. The sky that is. I've made you some cheese sandwiches and I've brought you a walking map. You'll need one.'

'We've got one of our own, actually,' said Rebecca. 'And, anyway, it doesn't look like it's going to clear. I think you're being a little over-optimistic on our behalf.'

'Oh, don't you worry, dear, it soon will,' said the farmer's wife. 'It always does.'

Jerry commented at half past eleven, when it did, that Mrs Ethel was clearly a clever woman full of local wisdom and added that it was a shame for the Ethels that they had such a simpleton for their only child. Rebecca demanded to know how Jerry could tell that the child was so simple and Jerry said it was because it hadn't said very much and had a gaga focus and couldn't Rebecca just stop being difficult about everything, please, because it was perfectly obvious it was defective and you could just tell.

'It's not an "it". He's a boy,' said Rebecca. 'And just because he doesn't talk much, that doesn't mean a thing.' On a practical note she chose to add that if he carried the torch then she would take the map.

Jerry rejoined that Rebecca, as she herself well knew from numerous trips they had made together to friends in Leytonstone, was a lousy mapreader. He told her that she could be in charge of the torch and he would be the one to navigate. He'd been in the boy scouts and he'd done geography O level. Rebecca felt emotional and tried hard not to burst into tears. She'd been expelled from the Brownies but she knew she could still deal with the Ordnance Survey.

'I'm sorry, you must have me confused with some other woman,' she said. 'This is your wife speaking and I did geography O level too, remember?'

'Oh, for God's sake, please don't start that again,' Jerry snapped as he dug out his Wellington boots. Sitting on the end of the bed to pull on his galoshes, he looked up and saw Rebecca placing a navy beret onto the crown of her head at half-tilt. She looked incredibly attractive, as always, and he wanted to touch her then and there. He walked over to his little wife and he enclosed her frail, knobbly hand in his. She was a delicate creature. Raising her raw skin to his lips, he kissed her pale palm and then he kissed it again. He stared into the pupils of her pained eyes and he couldn't feel any guilt. But he wanted to, he was trying hard. He would definitely sell his old flat in Camden when he got a proper offer. Absolutely definitely. It was only the market that was holding him back. He hardly ever used it any more anyway, so he didn't know why she made such a fuss. And he did feel sorry for her. She deserved better. He was a lousy husband, he knew, but what could you do?

'Come on, let's get out of here,' he said, his voice warm with affection, and, putting his arm around her shoulders, he led her out of the room, down the narrow, uneven stairs and out onto the rough, gravel path.

'Watch out for Ethel,' called out Mrs Ethel behind them. 'You might catch him up there with the sheep, on the ridge.'

Rebecca and Jerry turned and waved, holding hands firmly. Mrs Ethel waved back. She hoped that they wouldn't get lost. A lot of the Londoners had no sense of time or distance. They thought that nature was a challenge, something to be achieved. For Mr and Mrs Ethel it was a cold, wet way of making ends meet. But one that was more natural than sitting indoors on a swivel chair all day, moving a small, black cursor around a square orange screen. Mrs Ethel had seen a lot of couples like Rebecca and Jerry. They always came up to the Lake District on Fridays in early December to patch things up before facing unwanted relatives together over undesired chain-store socks on Christmas Day. She watched the couple treading their metropolitan path around moss-stagnating puddles and then she turned sharply and went back indoors to talk to Sam, her boyish-looking daughter.

Rebecca and Jerry breathlessly mounted the badly maintained path and strove to achieve the summit. And then they unpacked their small, neat rucksacks and, in their megabitten lives, filled with success and reward, they chose to award themselves a lunchbreak. Out came the plastic sandwiches. They sat in silence and Rebecca couldn't bear it.

'I'm having a miserable time,' she said.

cannes rendezvous

Jack had a new pupil. What he really wanted was to be able to label himself as something exciting, someone glamorous. When people at parties asked him 'What do you do?' he wished he could say that he was a – well, he didn't actually know, he couldn't think of anything. That was part of the problem. Or so Emily said. He couldn't visualise himself as anything more than a maths teacher. He had no imagination. But the truth was, he told her, that he enjoyed teaching.

Now Emily, on the other hand, was a jazz singer. That is to say, when people at parties asked her what she did for a living, she said, 'I'm a jazz singer.' Which wasn't strictly true. Because, actually, it was Jack who made the living and paid the rent. What Emily mostly did, on a day to day basis, was serve customers in the Pizza Parlour. It was quite a nice pizza parlour, mind, and Jack frequently picked up a slice of Napolitana with extra anchovies on the evenings that he went to pick up Emily from her evening shift, but the point was that most of the time Emily worked as a waitress.

There was nothing wrong with being a waitress. God, he'd be the last person to criticise someone for the way in which they made their daily garlic bread, but he did feel that it was just a little bit rough of Emily to carp on constantly about his humdrum, banal existence, when what she did for a living was a good deal less significant than educating the adults of tomorrow.

It was a bone of contention.

Every second Thursday, Emily came into her own. She would lie prone on a baby grand, at a local hotel, and belt out a few tunes accompanied by a mid-thirties man in a rather worn dinner jacket. She was quite good, actually. She sang Kurt Weill songs in the original German and wore a long, sequinned evening gown that was split all the way up the middle. When she swung round mid-note you could sometimes catch a glimpse of the top of her suspender belt. Emily thought it was sexy.

Just recently the management of the Hotel Cannes Rendezvous had been running short of guests so they'd decided to cut down on Emily's entertainment hours. Now they rang her up on spec whenever the bar was full and asked her to come on down and give them a few. The owner was a bit of a joker and he always expressed himself like that. Jack thought he was a right git but it was Emily's sole outlet as a performance artiste so he restrained himself. Emily said that you never knew. One day there might be someone really important staying at the hotel, an impresario or a theatrical agent or the manager of the London Palladium. Then she would be discovered and she'd never again have to sing with Mr Battle accompanying her on the piano. Jack chose not to comment. We're all entitled to our dreams.

Big Battle, they called him between themselves. He was massive. His dinner jacket was too small and the transparent jigger button at what used to be the waistline had fallen off so the jacket flapped a little loosely round the middle. Big Battle occasionally achieved victory over the notes. But not often. Big Battle turned around to the audience in the middle of songs and beamed a lot as he played, which Emily didn't like him to do since it meant that they caught sight of the large balls of tepid sweat dripping down his forehead. He tried terribly hard. He had trained in Melbourne at a proper musical school where they truly appreciated his talent. It wasn't the same now that he'd come back to England. It rained constantly, there wasn't much call for performance work and nobody clapped when he trilled with real bravado. In Australia they all applauded everything he did and nobody had called him 'Fatty'.

Jack and Emily thought Big Battle made that last bit up. It was impossible. He was the comic half of a double act – the Beast to Emily's Beauty. The audience loved it. Emily regularly sang 'Falling In Love Again' with a sensual, Teutonic accent as she dripped down the front of the baby grand and twirled her petite body around Mr Battle's big one, opening her eyes wide and gazing at him in adoration. The Italians at the bar pissed themselves laughing. The French men whistled. The English men were generally drunk and missed the entire act but they did sometimes sober up in time to get in a bit of heckling, using phrases like 'Oi, Fatty, I thought Pavarotti was a singer.' They loved that joke. Some of them came in regularly just to shout it out and humiliate Big Battle. Mr Battle didn't seem to notice the general public derision but Emily minded a lot. She thought it lowered the tone of the act and she had asked the manager on several occasions to clear the bar of all unseemly elements.

The manager had pointed out that alcohol was where the cash flow lay and she should bear that in mind next time she made a helpful suggestion that would cost him money since his biggest saving would be to get rid of the act completely. So Emily and Big Battle were trapped with the hecklers at the Hotel Cannes Rendezvous and Emily sunk her woes by learning the lyrics to all the parts in *The Threepenny Opera* in both English and German. She took the whole learning enterprise extremely seriously and treated it as a run-through of the big time, which, for her, it undoubtedly was.

'Mac the Knife,' she warbled as she pranced around the kitchen table. 'Mekky Messer,' she pronounced carefully.

'I'm not trying to put you off,' called out Jack from the living-room as he went through the maths exercise with Brian Severidge, 'but we are trying to fathom algebra in here. Perhaps you could go into the garden to do that or just stop for half an hour, please.'

'Go into the garden? What are you on about? It's freezing out there.' They went through this dialogue almost every evening. Tonight's audience happened to be Brian Severidge who was fourteen and had acne. Naturally, he fancied Emily like mad. Emily reckoned that three-quarters of Jack's pupils only turned up in the first place so that they could ogle her bosom whilst she did warm-up exercises on the kitchen table, which the boys could just about glimpse from the living-room table when the door was wide open, which was exactly how Emily always left it.

'It's sad, really,' commented Jack, 'it's sad that you need to justify yourself by swanning around half-naked in front of a thirteen-year-old. I call that really sad. And now Bob's starting lessons I hope you're not going to be dallying your goods in front of him. He, for one, might not like it.'

'I can't believe that,' claimed Emily. 'My cleavage keeps your business going; we're symbiotic, you and I. I'll bet this young Bob of yours will just adore all the peaks and troughs of my talents.'

'I doubt it,' said Jack, 'I very much doubt it'.

'We shall see,' Emily retorted, brazen challenge in her eyes.

At precisely seven PM, with leotard-wearing Emily keyed up in the kitchen, her tape recorder on the ready, Jack heard footsteps descending the stone stairs and approaching the front door of their basement flat. There was a ring at the bell. Emily grabbed a quick look in the mirror and, smoothing over her hair, struck a pose. Jack opened the door. And in walked Big Battle.

'What?' gasped Emily, who didn't know what the fuck B.B. suddenly wanted out of the blue like this but she was keen to get rid of him before Bob arrived. 'We're expecting someone,' she called out, rather sharply from the kitchen. 'We can't talk to you now, we're expecting Bob.'

'My beloved Emily,' said Jack patiently, 'it is only *I* who am expecting Bob, not *we*, and this, my friend, is he. Go back to your scullery corner, Cinderella, and perhaps one day you, too, will turn into a pumpkin.'

'I'm not going back in there,' cried Emily, 'I want to know what's going on. Mr Battle, or should I say "Bob",' she added tartly, 'what the hell are you doing here? You're a bloody pianist, for God's sake.'

Big Battle beamed at Emily, whose cleavage he had not noticed.

'I may be just a pianist to you,' he explained, 'but, in my own mind, I'm someone with the potential to pass maths O level. I want to better myself, Emily. I want to diversify. I've always had a mental block with academic studies. I failed maths O level four times so it's become a symbolic personal obstacle for me. I was chatting to Jack about it just last week after the show and we agreed that it's never too late to face one's personal challenges and they always begin with the little things. No point sitting at home wishing I could be a maths teacher. I'm going to meet my private goal head on. Jack can teach and I can learn. Maths GCSE is the obvious place for me to start the rest of my life. Fifth time round there'll be no luck involved. I'm telling you now, I'm no longer an "unclassified" kind of guy. I'll get at least a C. I will. And that's just the start of my

"Towards the Millennium" personal improvement programme. Emily, I'm so excited. I'm on my way.'

Emily had never seen B.B. so animated. It occurred to her that in all these years she had never even been aware that B.B.'s name was Bob.

'Do you two often talk to each other?' she asked, slightly petulant. And it transpired that they did. They sat down together on the imitation leather sofa in the bar while she was changing and they did quick crosswords and bought each other the odd gin and tonic in a plastic beaker and, quite often, they had a bit of a giggle over all the slobberingly drunken hotel folk at the bar.

How could I never have noticed? Emily thought, looking at the boys. What could I have been doing while all this friendship was going on? As the two men got out their graph paper, she closed the kitchen door behind her and went out into the garden to practise her scales.

dirty raincoats

There I was, just sitting around at home, feeling a little queasy and over-anxious about Paul's slightly deviant behaviour, when I caught sight of his raincoat. It was repellent to me. There was dirt all over the collar and a great muddy patch on the sleeve, as if he'd been on a ramble in the countryside, except that he can't have been because we don't like the countryside. We never go there.

I went over to the raincoat and picked it up tentatively, holding it well away from my highly trained professional nose. I would take it to the dry cleaner's in the morning, I thought, and this time

I would remember to check the pockets for forgotten dirty tissues before I went so that they would not become sodden and mashed to shreds in Mr Marvel's Clean Machine. And that was when it fell out and hit me right in the guts.

We are an independent couple. You must understand that I wouldn't normally dream of taking Paul's clothes to the cleaner's. We've always maintained a strictly Cook Your Own Bloody Dinner I've Got A Career Too kind of relationship and we make a big point of going on holiday at least once a year with just our own friends and not each other. Keeps the buzz going, we like to think, sustains our marriage where the alcohol doesn't help, that's the joke we make. We've always been just joking, you understand.

This year Felicity and Eliza and I all went on a tour of the lesser known parts of western Spain. Felicity fucked a waiter and Eliza got drunk in a disco in Santiago and took her top off to show the local lads her tattoo. Apparently they'd never seen a lady with a painted butterfly on her left breast before. Or so they told Eliza in order to encourage her to get her kit off. She didn't need much encouragement.

I've got a tattoo on the higher reaches of my right thigh, actually, because all three of us had them done last year on a wild weekend in Warsaw. You can't say we don't get around, the girls and I, and we always go to interesting, slightly off the wall places. There's absolutely nothing tacky about our girls' only getaways. But I chose not to reveal my upper thigh in Dance Heaven of Santiago. Felicity and Eliza teased me about this and said I'd lost my bottle and turned into a boring old fart but I told them to stop being both windist and ageist and, anyway, I wasn't in the mood so could they please just shut up and leave me alone.

You have to hand it to them, though, they really know how to enjoy themselves. With the passing of the years I have forgiven but never forgotten the fact that Eliza almost ruined my wedding day by making a pass at the best man before the service even began. She forcibly hauled him off into the bushes behind the church for a quick one while I had to sit in the car with my dad waiting for them both to reappear, looking flushed. We go back a long way, the girls and I.

The fun-filled fortnight of rhythmic thrusting at Dance Heaven was already long obliterated from my mind by the time we touched down in Horley at a very anti-social hour of the morning. The plane had been delayed for many hours so we all got compensatory tokens for free sausage and chips in the Gatwick Village but Paul was in a hurry to get to work so he drove us straight back to sodden Wandsworth, a gloomy place at the best of times. However, it had sprouted a drive-through McDonald's while we were abroad, and Eliza and Felicity got excited about this and, having already rebuked Paul for causing them to miss out on free chips, they made us park up and buy some from a cheeky chappy sporting a white paper hat and a badge with the word 'Don' on it, before they would permit Paul to drop us all off at our respective homes. Looking distinctly put upon, since he finds it hard to handle three women at once, he mumbled on about it being an important day at work and then zoomed off to deal with it. The girls may rip the piss out of my husband but I know they like getting lifts with him really; they were glad to be spotted by the white-paper-hat man in the back of a Porsche.

Paul normally comes home at about seven thirty. He works very hard, the girls surely can't deny that. This evening, though, he came in at six and my immediate reaction to this was, Oh wow, he's missed me, he's rushed all the way home early just to be with me because he's so excited to have me by his side. Shows how daft you can be really. Even as he jogged in through the front door, Paul started behaving in a rather dysfunctional way. He barged straight into the house with his sinewy arms stuck rigidly out in front of his spindly body and then he thrust the large, golden box of chocolates that they were supporting into my stomach.

'I didn't want to embarrass you in front of the girls,' he said, 'but I have to say that you're looking great.'

'I wouldn't have been embarrassed,' I replied. 'You know I would have loved it.' I can tell what you're thinking. None of this sounds particularly odd, it all sounds perfectly tedious and domestic so what's all the fuss about? The point is, that we've been married for three-and-a-half years. That's forty-four months. Not that I'm knocking marriage as an institution, God knows, you couldn't have a proper affair without it. But that's always been Felicity's little joke, never mine.

To get back to this box of chocolates, the weirdest aspect of the whole thing was that Paul came home, gave me this incredible box of chocolate truffles, told me I looked great and then left the house.

For a second I thought he was jogging back to the Porsche in the driveway to retrieve some other splendid token of his affection.

'Where are you going?' I said, beginning to suspect that this may not be the case. As I say, we respect each other's privacy, we both know you need personal space within a marriage or it will all collapse around you, but I found myself saying, despite my best intentions, 'Where are you going? I've got some champagne truffles to share and I've got no bikini lines.' I am well aware that one of the most unattractive qualities in the world is to need someone more than they need you, but I couldn't stop myself asking. I hadn't seen the guy for a fortnight, after all. And it wasn't me who removed my lycra crop top in a disco in Santiago. I'm a married woman, for God's sake, I have a husband.

But my husband has walked out of the door and has disappeared from sight. He has gone. I was more than a little upset about this marital vacuum and I therefore sat and hoovered every single one of the extremely expensive-looking chocolates without him and made myself sick. It was at this point in the evening that I noticed the dirty raincoat and decided to look, in all innocence, through its silk-lined pockets. I was not searching for evidence. Far from it. But, having found some, I can only conclude that my wretched git of a husband is having an affair.

I phoned Eliza. She was not in. Her answering machine told someone called Jerry that he absolutely had to wait for her because she was on her way and she would snog him something chronic when she arrived. How can she bring herself to leave messages like that? was what I thought, imagining my embarrassment if my grandmother or my bank manager were to ring and hear such a pile of drivel. I'd be mortified. I tried Felicity's number. Felicity's machine was also on but I spoke into it and said that it was only me and that if she were there she should pick up the phone now because this was an emergency and I should never, ever partner her in the Funky Chicken again if she didn't respond.

'So what's so important,' demanded Felicity, 'that I have to be interrupted mid-coital to talk to you? Shut up and bend over, Big Boy,' she added, for my amusement, no doubt. Who the hell was Big Boy? Why do all of my unmarried friends seem to be having so much more of a life than I do? Why?

'Get to the point, Big Tits,' said Felicity, 'there's some coming that needs to get going around here.' Felicity thought I was working myself up into a state about nothing. There was most likely some quite simple, unbearably tedious explanation. He'd got some business problem he didn't want to tell me about and he was softening the blow by buying some chocolates. He'd lost his job and his manhood had suffered a setback to its overweening, high-salary-earning pride. He couldn't face me, his delicate flower of a protectee, so he'd gone out into the cold of the night to pace the streets and mull over his humiliation as a man, his husbandly uselessness. He was wondering how to break the image-shattering news. Felicity has never liked Paul so I decided to ignore everything she had said. 'Hang on in there, Donga Doug,' she added, but I knew she had to be exaggerating.

'So,' I said, launching at the main stumbling block to her explanation, 'what have you got to say about the inside pocket discovery, then?' I demanded to know the answer. This could not be explained. I felt the quite unnecessary need to inform

Felicity that my life was quite as intricate and interesting as hers, and I bet I had sex on a more regular basis. She said she doubted that very much but, in any event, she was more concerned with quality than quantity. I was fairly annoyed with Felicity by this stage and I decided that I would make her pay me back the money she owed me for the pink fluorescent sombrero I bought her in Toledo. To add to her heap of vocal indignities Felicity didn't have anything constructive to add to my emotional crisis. Her only idea on the topic of the inside pocket was that Paul wanted to surprise me at the airport by throwing me over his shoulder, dragging me, Tarzan-like, to the mother and baby room and proceeding to fuck me senseless. He had brought with him the necessary precautions to prevent us needing the room for its designated purpose in the near future. I pointed out to Felicity that Paul hadn't fucked me senseless since 1986.

'And I think that's a highly unlikely explanation,' I added and I wondered why Felicity was using the opportunity to patronise me. Paul would never dream of taking me unawares on an airport floor. It would ruin his Paul Smith suit. She knew that. It was a constant barb of my friends that Paul was too vain for his own wardrobe. Nothing could do justice to his perfect form. They were jealous, I said, but I realised that it was me who was on the defensive.

'So, not to put too fine a point on the family planning,' finished Felicity, 'but that just about safely covers the wandering penis issue, don't you think? So, dig me, Doug, let's get down to business, let's move the earth.' And the old tractor rang off. I rang again but the machine was still on and, this time, she didn't pick up the phone.

'May you never achieve orgasm!' I screamed into the receiver and slammed it down in a rage. They always had to make a point, did my friends. Felicity doesn't even know anyone called Doug. You can say one thing for her, though. She doesn't let emotions get in the way of her relationships.

Okay, I thought, as I mulled over the evidence, so I made a

mistake. I married Paul. The guy's an arsehole. I wish I weren't married. But do they have to thrust it down my throat at every possible opportunity? Felicity and Eliza have a bloody good holiday every time we go away and I don't get to join in because I take my marital responsibilities seriously and I spend most of the time wishing I were with Paul and wondering what he's up to while I'm away and now I know and consequently I feel a bit bloody stupid. While I've been comporting myself like a nun on overtime in Spain, Paul's been wandering around Wandsworth buying packets of extra-fine protection and stuffing them firmly down the inside pocket of his dirty raincoat.

I sat down calmly and did the breathing exercises I had learned in ante-natal classes. I wasn't expecting a baby when I attended but I wanted to get a bit of early practice in and see whether the other women were worth getting to know. Maybe Felicity's explanation was right, I decided as I exhaled vigorously. After all, the packet was unopened. God, that would be even worse. Paul without a job. It was unthinkable.

I got the packet out of his pocket and I ripped it open, looking for inspiration. I removed the contents and stretched them lengthways and sideways above the table, tugging them in all directions. I held one to my mouth and blew it up into a contorted balloon shape which I then twisted into an unidentified zoo animal. I did the same thing to a second one and then placed the pair facing each other and made the two zoo animals kiss. I suddenly caught sight of myself in the living-room mirror and realised how stupid I looked. I would take the only practical course of action open to me. I made myself comfortable on the sofa and went to sleep.

'Darling,' Paul said, waking me brusquely to a pitch black night hours later. 'Please do tell me why there are two inflated condoms on our living-room table?'

'Darling,' I replied sweetly, 'hasn't anyone ever told you that two dickheads are better than one?'

Paul was looking particularly smooth this evening, he

thought. He was wearing his brushed cotton paisley shirt and his purple leather jacket with all the zips. He volunteered no information as to his recent whereabouts. Instead he informed me that my joke wasn't funny and that I should do some serious work on the punchline if I was thinking about using it on members of the general public.

'Okay, you humourless smartass,' I said, reaching for the confrontation. 'Is there anything you'd like to tell me now? Anything about extra-domestic country rambles you've been taking lately?'

'We hate the countryside,' he said. 'We never go there. What exactly are you getting at with these snide rural comments?'

'Aha,' I said, 'you're on the defensive already, it's all becoming transparently clear.'

'Defensive?' said Paul. 'I'm not being defensive. How on earth could I be defensive? I don't have a clue what you're talking about.'

'If that's the case,' I said, pointing triumphantly at the two deformed and stinking rubber zebras lying buoyantly on the glass-topped table, 'what have you got to say about those?'

'I think,' he said, in his irritatingly considered and reflective way, 'that it would be more appropriate for you to tell me the answer to that question.'

'Very clever,' I said, 'very, very smart. But don't think you can wriggle out of this by being reasonable. Just you tell me right now, you fuckwit, what those contraceptive devices were doing in your dirty raincoat while I was boogieing away in Spain, you, you creepy creep.'

Paul hesitated and stepped towards me, maintaining his loveable but naughty schoolboy expression and crinkling his lower lip. There was a moment's silence while we stared at each other and I thought about how strange it was that you can know someone so well and yet be suddenly so totally separate from them in every way.

I lost my cool. I got upset. I sat down on the sofa and looked as if I might cry. Paul looked shifty.

'God, don't do that,' he said, impotently, 'you always burst into tears when I'm trying to tell you something important.'

My heart sank. Now that the moment had come, I no longer wanted to confront the issue. I hadn't asked a precise question deliberately because I hadn't wanted to hear a specific answer. But now I braced myself for the information I was about to receive.

'I was going to tell you straightaway,' he said, looking rueful, 'but I just couldn't break the news to you in front of Felicity and Eliza.'

'Just spit it out,' I said, because at least I could punish him to the extent of making him vocalise his wrong-doings.

'I didn't know how to tell you,' he said, 'so I'm just going to say it straight up. At work I've been put in charge of the condom account. That's it. I've been promoted. I've been made a partner and I have to advertise rubbers. I've landed the biggest campaign of the season. I didn't mention it before because I knew the girls would laugh at me and at my values in life and that would have ruined the moment for both of us but, now, I'm going to do a jig around the living-room and then we can start doing some serious training for the campaign. So let's get the show on the road by smearing each other with chocolate truffles, shall we?'

He let out a yelp and yodelled round the coffee table like a village idiot, chucking the wilting zebras into the air and squeaking away like a blooming moron. I was thrilled. Felicity and Eliza would be gutted. And instead of Paul dying of shame, it was me. We tumbled down onto the shag-piled floor and Paul fucked me senseless, but I'd eaten far too many chocolates and I threw up at half-time.

'I'll bet Donga Doug wouldn't wipe up Felicity's vomit,' I said to Paul as we reached for another zebra.

'Who's Donga Doug?' he said.

eliza and jerry go out on a date

'Eliza and Jerry go out on a date,
He may not yet know but he's her
perfect mate'

What do you mean, you don't get it? It's a bloody poem for God's sake, what is there to get? Well, I know it doesn't quite scan but I felt so uplifted about the whole incident that I just had to write a little ditty to celebrate my love. What are you talking about? Are you kidding? Of course we did. Every day a best knicker day, that's me. No, hang on a minute, I have to tell it all in the right order, I don't want to spoil the story. Hey, you haven't got me on that monitor device, have you, so old Loopy Loo can hear? She already thinks we must be lovers the amount I ring you. Last time I came in to meet you for lunch she gave me a very significant look and said it was okay by her, she was very broad-minded. Well, I know, but sometimes your sense of humour is lost on me.

Anyway, more important, what's the Bobby Moore with you and Dudley? Oh sorry, Doug then, how'd it go with Doug? Really. God that's good going for a first sexual encounter. Really. Bloody Hell. And from behind. Blimey. He seemed to be into that one, did he? I say, Felicity, every day at least a *three* best pairs of knickers day for you at the moment. Steady on, my friend. If Loopy Loo hears you talking like that she'll be breaking the hinges on her swivel chair. Oh, so you're allowed fag breaks in your industrial Bastille, are you? Where do you go to smoke, then? No, of course I don't mean you, I mean where does Loopy Loo go when she has a fag break? Right, so she can't hear any of this conversation then. Good, let's hear it, then.

Right, so you stayed the night, did you? Had a good, hard bed, did he? A futon. Impressive stuff. The guy's a serious contender, then. Christ Almighty. All night. God, where do you find these men? The ones I pick up have problems locating their own sexual organs let alone inserting them into mine.

Mmm, I know what you mean, that always is a bit of a disappointment. It's the taste that puts me off.

Look, to get back to more important things, I have to tell you all about my hot date with Jerry. Yes, you remember him, that guy from the advert. No not that one. No, that one was really boring and I reckon he lives with his girlfriend. He wanted us to break into his office in the middle of the night and do it on his boss's VDU. Yes, really. No, I didn't get it either. You'd need to be a contortionist to sustain that as a sexual position. But, listen, wait until you hear about Jiving Jerry.

Yes, that's right, the one that wrote the really sweet letter about his dog and all that. No, you're getting them all mixed up, not him. Well, yes, I did ring that one up but he gave me this really long sob story about why he's not the kind of guy who would ever normally dream of answering an advert in *Time Out* but his wife had just left him, and his pet lizard had been devoured by his neighbour's cat, and he'd had a run of bad luck, but it was all coming together for him now, and he wanted someone special to share it all with. Yes, I agree, that bit turned me right off, too. And that's exactly what I said, actually. No, he didn't take it too well. He hung up so I decided he was a dead loss and I never rang him again.

Anyway, this one says he runs a PR agency. He was really, really normal sounding. He wrote me this letter, with a rather sexy photo and it was pretty short and correctly punctuated. No, I know it's not important in the early stages but if he turned out to be fabulous and we got to the love letters stage it would be a real blow not to be able to show them off to all your friends cos they were so badly written. So, okay, I might be jumping the gun a bit, but if all I wanted was a quick shag I would hardly need to pay thirty-five quid for a box space, would I?

So this photo was really cute and he's got blond hair and he's from Gunnersbury but lives in Camden, both of which are on the North London Line, and I always feel that's a very good omen. Well, it was really simple, sort of sophisticated. He said he works very hard, he leads a busy life and, although he has a lot of friends, he just never has the opportunity to meet new people outside of work. He wanted to extend his social life, in fact just having a social life would do. Yes, I thought that was a nice touch, too, sort of humble, isn't it? No, I don't think so. Well, I was hardly going to ask him, was I?

So I was pretty excited about this date with Jerry. We arranged to meet in that new bar underneath Sainsbury's with the weird wire tree in the window and the rather sexy waiter that Madeleine once fucked. No, he didn't seem to be there any more, it's a woman now. I thought that was a shame, too.

I went in and looked around and there was only one guy sitting by himself at a table and he was absolutely gorgeous. I mean, seriously hot stuff, so I knew that it couldn't possibly be him, but I thought I should profit from the occasion so I went over and asked him if he wasn't, by any chance, Jerry? Because, if so, I was Tom. I know it's really stupid, but I was a bit nervous, and, anyway, it's endearingly feminine, isn't it? Too gauche to be brazenly forward.

Well, that's the whole point. It was him, Jerry. I couldn't believe it. That was my immediate reaction, too, but why should he? He was the best-looking guy in the bar. He didn't need to pick anyone up by telling a stupid lie. No, that was my second reaction, but then, even if it had been a coincidence, he would have known he wasn't meeting a girl called Eliza, wouldn't he?

He was so dead cool. He had real Restaurant Presence. He barely needed to glance upwards before the waitress came rushing over to take the order. A Budweiser. I had a Sol. I know it's naff but I was feeling premenstrual so I said the first thing that came into my head. God, I might have asked for something really uncool like a mug of hot chocolate, the mood I was in.

Anyway, the Sol arrived very promptly with the requisite slice of lime perched on the edge of the bottle and I pushed it down the neck. I didn't squeeze it. I felt like I was doing okay, and it was a stroke of luck, actually, because it meant we didn't have to think up anything. There it was mangled in the neck of the bottle-conditioned beer right in front of my nose. Crap. I'm not being obscure. Like I told you, he runs this PR agency and they'd just been doing a lime campaign. He knew everything there was to know about limes. Oh, loads of interesting things, I can't remember now, I wasn't listening, actually, I was just staring at him thinking, fucking hell, how come a guy as totally fucking Adonis-like as yourself needs to answer an advert in *Time Out*? Of course I didn't bloody ask him, you think I'm soft in the head or something? No, he just loved it. I sat there, gob-smacked, staring at him. He clearly thought he was desperately clever and entertaining and that was where the pull lay for him. All the other girls admired his looks, no doubt, but I was really after his brain. I know. I followed your Plan A and it worked. When in doubt, say nothing. I was an audience of one and I kept all my options open.

Yes, not surprisingly that's exactly what I asked, but funnily enough, it being the only interesting thing there is to find out about limes, he didn't know the answer. He said he'd never thought about citrus fruit in those terms before, he was merely in the business of promoting his product. Are you kidding? I was hardly going to get into an ethics debate with a guy I wanted to shag.

I can't really remember, let's see, he told me that he'd lived with a girl once but they got bored with each other, or something like that. No, I didn't say anything, I wasn't going to get into that shit. I changed the subject to the guacamole in front of us and, rather enterprisingly I thought, he started talking about the anthropology of food. He'd been reading a book about table manners and he told me at great length about the history of chicken as Sunday lunch. Well, what was I supposed to do? I acted impressed. No, of course not, I didn't want to scare the guy off so I just tried to look as if it was hot news to me. Well, yes, it was all just a trifle embarrassing, because then he said he didn't want to go for that obvious one, but now that I knew all about his job, I shouldn't hold out on him any longer and so what did I do to earn my daily crust?

I wasn't going to lie. I thought he carried it off quite well, actually. He just asked me why I hadn't mentioned it earlier because I must know an awful lot more about the whole subject than he did. I just said, well, anthropology is a big field and food wasn't really my specialist area and, anyway, it was always interesting to listen to a layperson's views. Mmm. Well, it did put a bit of a dampener on the conversation so I just made a bad joke and said that since he lived nearby, maybe we could go back to his place and I could enlighten him about the anthropology of the coffee bean in his own home. Well, what the fuck, if I'd wanted to talk poultry, I could have stayed at work for the evening. It was his turn to look a bit nervous. He said he didn't think he'd ever been on a blind date with a lecturer before and he hoped I wasn't inviting myself in for a spot of intellectual domination. Yes, I thought that was more than a trifle suggestive, also. I guessed I was home and wet by this stage so I said, no, it was more the physical kind that I had in mind. He looked a bit shocked – well, that's an exaggeration – he raised his eyebrows quizzically and then, with the incandescent RP he had demonstrated earlier, he raised his little finger and the waitress instantaneously jogged over with the bill. He laid a ten-pound note on the saucer and he said, 'So let's go and do some domination practice, shall we?'

I thought it was all incredibly sexy. I was beside myself with anticipation at this point. We walked over to his flat. We didn't say much, just sort of swung our limbs about in a highly synchronised way, frissons of erotic tension criss-crossing the pavement between us.

His flat was only across the road. It was decorated in white with a great big, framed blow-up of an incredibly beautiful girl on the living-room wall. She was kind of suspended doing the splits in mid-air above what looked like a tropical beach. He saw me staring at the photo, which you couldn't avoid doing since it was the most noticeable thing in the room, and he told me that it was his old girlfriend, the one he'd been telling me about in the bar. I said, right, right, attractive girl, attempting to sound aesthetically objective and big-minded but I didn't think things were looking too hopeful at this stage in the evening. I sat down on the sofa and he went into the kitchen to make us both some strong, dark Arabic coffee.

As soon as he was gone I got up again and had a nose around the living-room. On the fitted shelves there were a couple of coffee-table books about the Post-Impressionists, some manuals on marketing strategy, an object that looked like it might be a strobe machine and an illustrated *Karma Sutra*. There were also two photos in rather beautiful marquetry frames. One was of an old couple in front of a boring-looking brick house, the other of a young baby, no clues as to whose. The walls were stark white apart from this big poster of the flying fancy girl. Oh yes, and there was also a framed poster of an advert for limes. I suppose that it was all quite tasteful in a businesslike kind of way.

I had ages to look around since he was taking an inordinate length of time just to make a simple cup of coffee. I began to get nervous sitting there, looking gormless, and, much as I wanted to be striking a considered and sophisticated pose when Jerry came back into the room, I'd already studied everything in it several times over and I couldn't hold on to the lime-flavoured contents of my bladder any longer. I found the bathroom quite easily but there was no lock when I got inside, so I just closed the door firmly and tried to keep relief snappy.

Then, as I was sitting there, taking a leak, the door suddenly opened so fast that I couldn't do anything to prevent it and the guy just sauntered on in. It was unreal, but to make matters worse, he had no clothes on. No, I mean no clothes at all, not a stitch. He barged his way past me, still sitting on the toilet doing my pee, threw himself onto his back on the floor and then just lay there, horizontal, with me still sedentary, my knickers halfway down my legs, and then, and this is the really freaky part, he was lying there, stark bollock naked, on his bathroom floor, when he suddenly uttered the words, '*Piss on me, baby.*'

Well, what could I do? I was simply astonished. It was quite extraordinary. No wonder the guy answers adverts in magazines. No wonder Miss Fancy learned to fly away. No, of course, I didn't. I mean, I'd only just met the guy. It may be a well-known fetish in Wandsworth but I was in Camden in some total stranger's bathroom, with his naked dick sticking straight upwards somewhere around my ankles.

I thought I was just great. I finished my pee. I rose, I pulled my best knickers up, I went over to him and I knelt down seductively near his face. And then I whispered into his ear in a highly sensual way that I was quite happy to have straight sex with him then and there but I didn't really feel that mutual urination was appropriate behaviour for one's first sexual encounter together. Then I got up and I walked out of the bathroom leaving him ample opportunity to do whatever he needed to do while I got my coat from the living-room and made ready to leave. He didn't seem to be emerging from the bathroom in any kind of hurry so I got my lipstick out of my coat pocket and, in big, scarlet figures all over the photo of the Flying Fancy, I scrawled my number. And then I left.

Isn't it just? One fuck of a story. No, not yet. But it was only the other day. Are you kidding? Of course I want to see him again. I've heard that urine is very good for the skin. Yes, that's exactly what crossed my mind, actually, no wonder he waited to do it in his marble-floored bathroom, he's the kind of guy who'd hate to ruin his living-room carpet.

Loopy Loo back now, is she? That was hardly a fag break, more of a cancer ward promotion morning. Well, look I really better ring off because it's an expensive time of day and this is the faculty phone after all. So what are you doing this evening, then? Doug again, eh? It'll burn out if you carry on like that. Maybe you could try pissing on him, that should dampen his ardour. Of course I'm being facetious. I hope it goes really well. No, now that you've stood me up, I think I'll just stay in and compose a few more poems for Jerry, while I wait for him to call. Of course I want him to, I have sand-blasted floorboards, remember?

felicity's friend

Felicity had a friend whose professional name was Mr Whippy. Felicity was very proud that she knew someone with such enormous power to blackmail his clientele. Mr Whippy had three flats in London alone, each with a different decor to suit the individual requirements of his diverse customers, of whom he had many, since it was a well-known fact around town that he was the most talented whipper in the whole metropolitan area.

Felicity thought her friend was great. Every so often he would ring her up from his cellphone and describe the view from a yacht in the South Pacific or a beach cabin on the East African coast where he would be treating a captain of industry to the low-life delights of back weals and scored flesh. It was a very highly skilled profession. There were not many people who could perform the act with such sleight of wrist as he. And what's more he got an awful lot of job fulfilment. Which he very much enjoyed sharing with Felicity. It would be no lie to say that Mr Whippy was not discreet. And neither was Felicity.

On that first innovative evening, as Felicity was picking herself up from the floor after a failed attempt at a particularly novel sexual position with her new-found lover, Donga Doug, Doug made a rather feeble attempt at beating her with a string of rosary beads. Felicity thought it was all rather pathetic and her response, as she rubbed on the witch-hazel in what she hoped was a highly erotic manner, was that if Doug really wanted to get to grips with consensual beating he should meet her friend Mr Whippy and see how that grabbed him. Doug was pretty grabbed. He wanted to know all about Felicity's friend: how Mr Whippy bound up his clients in leather thonging, what sort of outfits he wore to do so, how he managed to whip them for a whole thirty minutes without really hurting them, and then, how, with a dramatic flourish towards the end of each session, he would suddenly turn on the power and, just for a few seconds, inflict genuine pain while the client achieved a truly earth-shattering climax. Or so Mr Whippy would have it.

Doug was fascinated. Felicity's purpose in narrating the anecdote was to encourage Donga Doug to try out some flagellation on her enticing form, but what Doug wanted most, on hearing the information, were names.

'Oh,' Felicity assured him, 'everyone always asks that. But it's not a secret, he doesn't give a shit, he'll tell anyone. You'd always think someone would try and sell that stuff to the tabloids but Mr Whippy says that no one's interested. They don't like the gay angle, that's what he says, it doesn't sell.'

Knowing that there was little he could usefully do with the

names of anonymous men of means, and using some narrative licence of her own, just for dramatic effect, Felicity reeled off a list of illustrious, high-earning names. She was keen to entertain Doug whose sexual prowess was, quite simply, unsurpassed in her very considerable experience. Felicity was happy. Doug was delighted and they went straight back to bed to practise the reverse wheelbarrow.

Doug genuinely liked Felicity. They had finally got it together at the birthday party of a mutual dope dealer. As Felicity walked in, she spotted Doug in the heavies' corner by the bathroom, snorting a line, and Felicity immediately crossed the soirée in her leather shorts and waistcoat outfit and asked if she could do some, too. Doug was only slightly out of his head and immediately handed her the plate and the fiver. Ten minutes later, noses dribbling, they left the party together and by the time they got back to his flat Felicity had already divested Doug of his acid-coloured T-shirt and groovy baseball cap. They forgot the cap in the taxi and the driver later gave it as a gift to one of the local boys who carried his luggage for him whilst he climbed Mount Kilimanjaro.

Doug, shirtless, was even better than Doug clothed. He had a hairy chest and red jeans. He was totally out of his head and took hours to come, which was fortuitous for Felicity as she always found it hard to achieve orgasm on a first sexual encounter. They were giggling and larking about and Felicity said that she was jealous because Doug's tits were bigger than hers, he really had to admit that he was a bit of a porker. Doug got a bit sniffy about this but they had a whole extra line each at that point in the proceedings and this time they didn't take it up the nose. The whole evening had a street value of over a hundred and fifty quid but, as they both later agreed, it was one fuck of an evening. Seventeen hours of foreplay and they were still gagging for penalty points. Only exhaustion prevented play. It's a game of two halves, they said to each other, as they went for interval slices of orange with the score at four all. Towards the end of the match Doug hit an own goal but

Felicity took it in good humour and said it was okay, he would always be a Premier League player to her. It was all looking good, feeling great right then. Match of the week.

But, on their second rendezvous, when they both felt as sick as a parrot, had run out of Charlie and were compelled to start relying on conversation as an aphrodisiac, Felicity resorted to telling Doug even more about her friend, Mr Whippy. It had always worked before.

That night Doug didn't stay. Post-wheelbarrow, he sprang out of bed and looked highly charged. Felicity thought it was the passion she inspired.

'Hey, you haven't seen my baseball cap around anywhere, have you?' he asked her. But she was practising vaginal exercises and didn't hear him. By the time she'd counted to twenty he had gone.

The next morning, she went round to Eliza's for breakfast. Eliza had taken the morning off work because she was in love. Felicity didn't ever bother to go in to the office on a regular basis as she didn't take her job as cost-efficiency routes' planner for the dustbin vans of Wandsworth Council very seriously. In any case, she couldn't face her office mate, Loopy Loo, and the eternally squeaking swivel chair on which Loo sat and eavesdropped on Felicity's more interesting telephone conversations.

Both Eliza and Felicity were looking rough. They gave their old friend Madeleine a ring. She was really full of herself and very keen to come over for a confab. She ran her own highly successful business from home, matching top-notch ladies to their perfect perfume, so she could organise her own work schedule. With the triumvirate complete, the women sat around the kitchen table looking like beached whales. Eliza frothed the cappuccino and put some half-prebaked croissants into the oven. Theirs was a meditative silence only broken by Felicity's groaned comment that this was just like the old days, with all three of them totally shagged out. Eliza said that she thought she was suffering from the ovary pain again and she would soon have to go back to the homoeopath. Felicity said she got that too sometimes and it was to do with the womb getting older, craving a pregnancy and not being able to perform its natural breeding function. Madeleine said that her and Paul were thinking about becoming imminent breeders. He'd been made a partner at work. Oh, said the girls, neither of whom were at all interested in Madeleine's husband since he had never shown the slightest inclination to lend them his sports car. Instead, they focused their attention on the day's papers, every single one of which Madeleine had picked up on the way over to Eliza's. They drew a tabloid and a serious journal each from the pile and spread them out between the mugs of coffee and the pots of jam and the hazelnut chocolate spread for which Eliza had a particular penchant.

Eliza looked at the front page of her newspaper and, facing her, in big, brazen headlines all the way across the top, she saw the words 'THREE LINE WHIPPING FOR CABINET MEMBERS' and then underneath in smaller print 'Top industrialists take a beating'. And there, right there, in the middle of the page, was a great big, black and white, telephoto lens image of Felicity's friend.

'Blimey,' said Eliza, 'it's your mate featured on the front page of the *Daily Disaster*.' They all stared at the smiling face of Mr Whippy. Felicity was devastated. She realised immediately that it could only be Donga Doug, her lover, who had given away the game. All the time she had been thinking it was a match made in heaven, he'd been thinking that it was a match made in hard currency. She was a kind girl. Her first thoughts were for Mr Whippy. How could she ever make it up to him. This was quite, quite awful.

'Forget Mr Whippy for the minute,' said Madeleine, rubbing the salt into the wound. 'What on earth does this tell you about your relationship with Donga Doug?' Madeleine was feeling just a little bit superior about the demonstrative superficiality of Felicity's friendships in comparison to her own marital bliss. The other girls might laugh at the conventionality of the relationship but the product of her and Paul's ineffable love would be little humans not newspaper articles.

Madeleine scoured the page for further dirt and then turned to page four for more. All three women gasped in astonishment as they stared at a double-page spread displaying around fifty passport-type photos of upstanding and righteous members of the establishment. The faces of all kinds of prominent people were staring blankly back at them, but they did have something in common. Every single one was male.

'I can't believe it,' said Felicity. 'I can see the evidence but it's impossible. I mean, I'm quite happy to admit that I told Doug about this chap and this one but I never said anything about any MPs, and I don't even know who this man is.' Felicity was stunned. But Eliza was speechless.

Mute, she pointed at a fuzzy photo four columns along and three photos down. She couldn't say a word. She just held out her paralysed finger above the poor quality print. The others stared at her and at the photo. It didn't look like her father; it was far too good-looking to be her MP, but it wasn't anyone they'd ever seen before. Felicity poured more coffee whilst Eliza recovered her voice from somewhere below her heart.

'That man,' she said at last, her stomach churning uncontrollably, 'that man there is the gorgeous Jerry, my true love, the potato in my jacket, the biobaby in my Swiss Cheese. I don't know what to say. I am devastated. I met a man, I fell in love and now my heart is broken. All in a week. I simply can't believe that he's into all that stuff and yet he didn't want to try it out on me.'

The girls were relieved. They comforted Eliza with the tender notion that she had, after all, only met him the once. And he never rang her back. And he hadn't lied to her since he clearly was called Jerry and he did run a PR agency. So, all things considered, you couldn't say that he wasn't a man of some integrity. Eliza was gloomy, contemplating the thirty-five pounds she would have to spend to renew her Lonelyhearts box number in *Time Out*. She stared at her fat-filled, crumbling croissant whilst Felicity went over to the telephone to make a long-distance call. Profound guilt weighed heavily upon her soul and she thought it might assuage her conscience to apologise profusely to Mr Whippy at peak rate on Eliza's telephone.

From somewhere in the swampy depths of the Florida Keys Mr Whippy picked up the receiver and Felicity said, 'My old friend, my disco dancing buddy, I don't know what to say to you. How can I begin to express how sorry I am.'

'What are you talking about, sweetie?' said Mr Whippy. 'I am absolutely delighted. Bunch of scumbags, the whole lot of them. I've been trying to sell that rubbish for years. I would have given the information away just to show up some of those hypocritical arseholes. And the ones you made up! Man, what a creative genius you are. I've told you for years that your talents are wasted on dustbin routings. I couldn't have done a better job myself. They'll never get anyone to give evidence against me and, with all the money I'm about to make from the new clients who'll come rolling in because of the scandal, I'm going to set up a manatee protection reserve right here in the Keys. And you couldn't possibly have given me a greater publicity boost to get the whole campaign going. I will love you forever for this and I assure you that I'm going to name the first adopted manatee after you. I can only say that I consider it an honour and a privilege to call myself Felicity's Friend.'

holding on

Yes, thank you, I am still holding. Well, look, maybe you could just give me an idea how long she'll be. I mean, what do you think, is it worth it? Yes, I fully appreciate that, but, well, oh all right then, I'll carry on holding for a little while. No, that's okay, I do realise that it's not your fault, but I have been trying to get through for about twenty minutes now. Yes, I know this is a busy time of day but I did try this morning, actually, and there was no one available to take my call then either. An automatic voice told me, in fact. Well, all I can say is that I'm sorry if it sounds that way and I'm really not blaming you for this . . . this . . . charade, but, to be perfectly frank with you, it's just that I'm beginning to wonder if there even is a Refuse Planning Officer in Wandsworth. Listen, I'm not going to get into an argument with you about her official title. If she wants to call herself the Cost Efficiency Routes' Planning Officer then I'm quite happy to call her that but, quite honestly, as things stand, I'd be amazed if I get to call her anything at all.

I mean, have you ever seen her? Has anyone in your office ever set eyes on the elusive Ms Felicity Flower? Does Interpol, perhaps, possess a Photo-fit description of her?

No, I'm really not trying to be funny, no, but I am beginning to get just a little bit cheesed off, I really am. Maybe you could just put me through to someone else who might be able to discuss the matter with me. I really don't want to be rude or anything but I did go through this whole thing with you from beginning to end once already today. Just about half an hour ago when I first started holding. Yes, that's right. The load of old rubbish. Yes, that was me. It's all coming back to you now, is it? No, I'm not being in the least bit sarcastic.

No.

Yes.

Well, as I'm sure I don't need to remind you, what happened was that I put my black plastic bag of rubbish out on the Wednesday evening but the dustbin van doesn't come until Friday morning. Then it turns out that you have this team of round-the-clock hound-dog inspectors who go sleuthing around the streets of Battersea, playing virtual reality Cluedo and sniffing out the miserable citizens who put out their rubbish on days which are unacceptable to the illustrious members of Wandsworth Borough Council. When the lugubrious Morse finds any evidence of this appalling, anti-social behaviour, he opens up the rubbish and tips the contents out all over one of Wandsworth's public highways in order to establish its former owner.

In my case, apparently, Super Sherlock concluded that the

garbage was mine because he discovered an envelope with my name and address on it. This quite staggering piece of investigative analysis, I might add, was not unassisted by the fact that, before he deposited its stinking contents onto my steps, the bag was sitting happily outside my own front door, minding its own business, and had Poirot and his conscientious colleagues taken the time to ring the bell, I would happily have acknowledged its contents to be mine. But no. Instead he opts to go marching off, brandishing my mangled, egg-stained envelope in his great, sweaty palm and, not a week later, what should I receive in the post but a photocopy of this very same epistle with 'NOTICE TO APPEAR' stamped all over it and a map telling me how to get to South-Western Magistrates' Court in order to make amends for my truly heinous misdemeanours.

What can I say? Arrest me, officer, in the name of the law. I hold my hands up in shame and wish to atone for my seriously disturbed behaviour. Please, please, throw away yet more taxpayers' money by pursuing more hopeless, destructive members of the local community just like me. My personal detritus remained abandoned for a whole twenty-four hours outside my own front door where it disturbed no one but my family and myself in a most inconsiderate way and now, I fear, you must punish me in a way commensurate to my abysmal behaviour. Sentence me to an indefinite period of Community Service, I beg you, and let me spend the rest of my forties sweeping all the streets of Wandsworth in turn, single-handed, so that your Incredible Shrinking Routes' Planning Officer is rendered entirely redundant and spends the rest of her working career doing what she is clearly best at.

Hello? Hello, are you still there? Oh, hello. Sorry, no, I didn't mean to shout at you but, for one terrible moment there, I thought I'd lost you forever and I was so enjoying talking to you. No, I am, indeed, still holding on. Well, you don't have any way of telling, do you? I mean, whether she's still alive or not. No, it's okay, that was a joke. Yes, I do realise that you're only doing your job, but I'm sure you must realise how frustrating this all is for me. You don't have to tell me, I know just how you feel, I know, oh, I know.

Really? And how are they responding to the interminable wait, all these other people, who have, might I say, shown remarkably long-suffering patience, hanging on for all these decades. Well, it's not really that surprising, wouldn't you agree? Yes, I can well understand that it probably isn't pleasant to be in your shoes and of course you're doing your very best, but whose fault, might I enquire, is that? I'm sorry, I didn't quite catch that. Really? That's so, is it? I'm not being rude when I say that I'm not surprised. I might even believe you. I have tried ringing in the early morning on Tuesdays, at lunchtime on Wednesdays, all day on Thursdays, on spec on Saturdays, and, indeed, in the early hours of the morning on Sundays, when I'm lying awake, suffering from insomnia and worrying about the effect that a criminal record will have on my career. What I can't understand is why the hell this woman doesn't get the sack, then, if what you're saying is true? She never appears in the office, she never does any work, she never answers her phone and, from what I understand, no one can bear to spend more than ten minutes at a time with the blasted woman.

I don't want to bore you by going on about this, heaven save us, but, let's face it, everybody seems to know that she's nothing but a waste of space and, you have to admit, I'm paying good poll tax to keep sloths like her unemployed. Well, yes, I know we don't actually pay any poll tax in Wandsworth but it's the principle of the thing, is it not? Were I living in Lambeth, for example, this would be an absolute outrage. Oh dear, I am sorry to hear that. Well, don't lose heart, you might grow up to marry a rich man and move to Westminster.

Look, to get back to the point, what I want to know is why the hell doesn't she get the sack, then, if she's so inefficient? I mean answer me that one, if you can. Is that it? I should have guessed. I really should have guessed. Oh my word, it makes you sick, doesn't it? God, it makes you want to jump up and down and punch the nearest man in the face. And to think that the rest of us have to struggle and fight and work our way up the ladder like decent human beings and no one gives us anything for nothing in this world and then look what we're up against. It makes you want to give up before you start, it really does. And I'll bet she's not even interested in him, right? You see, what did I say? It's the same old story. It's not who you know, it's who you fancy.

Take my boss, for example. He fancies my assistant and she constantly gets special bonus perks. And what do I get? Excuse my language, but bugger all. Not that I'm bitter by any means, good luck to her, that's what I say, but I'll bet this one's got long, blonde hair cascading down her shoulders and she doesn't even notice he exists, right? I knew it. I bloody knew it. And I bet she's constantly going on about how fat she looks, whilst she's pigging out on chocolate and still fits snugly into her genuine size eight mini-clothes. I knew it. God, it makes me want to buy the peroxide factory and just blow it up. Oh, really, are you? Really. Yes but natural is so different, don't you think?

But where does it leave the old hags like us, that's what I want to know? No, I certainly didn't mean to imply that thirty is old because it's not, it's very young, you've got your whole life ahead of you, I'm sure, but, well, here we are, the two of us, you, getting on a bit, although you're still a natural blonde, of course, and me, just beginning to use all the anti-wrinkle massage brushes that keep your sagging parts at bay, although Arnold, that's my husband, does say that I still have a great figure for a woman of my age, but what the hell does he know, anyway, and the point is, well, the point is, how can we compete with women like that? And I'll bet he sends her internal memos all the time, right? I can see it now. Bearing ridiculous, delinquent messages like 'Miss Flower, please shower me with your powerful bouquet.' God, I can't bear it. It just makes me want to . . . to . . . ooooh Lord, it does.

God, that is so true. It does make a pleasant change to have someone taking an interest in all my rubbish, I must say. What is your name by the way? Tina, that's funny, my daughter's called Tina, seven next month actually. No, only the one. Oh yes, I do agree, it is a nice age. She doesn't put her finger in the phone socket any more and cut me off when I'm trying to talk to my friends. I don't know yet, we haven't decided. She fancies a matching place set from the Disney Shop, with the glittery stuff that spins round the edge in the water or a hairdryer with some nozzles but Arnold is very keen to buy some video games. God, I don't know, you know what men are like, buying things they really want for themselves. It's the one where you make a little green monster jump off a cliff and rescue the Prince of Darkness, I think. You're so right. But what can I do? My husband gets these things into his head and then, well, as I say, you know what men are like about presents, I'm sure I don't have to tell you. Really? Oh dear, I am sorry to hear that. Well, at least you won't have to worry about what he's getting your kids for Christmas, then. I am sorry, that was a bit tactless of me, it just sort of slipped out. I can be like that sometimes, I know it's awful.

Look, never mind, Tina, I can call you Tina, can't I? There are always plenty more fish in the sea, that's what I say to Arnold every time he goes on about the enormous phone bill. And never forget, love, blondes do have a colour advantage. Well, I did guess as much, actually, although I didn't like to say so earlier, but now that I feel we know each other a bit better, I'll give you a word of advice. Never lie about the little things, Tina, because people will always spot the roots growing out in the end.

Oh yes, sorry about that, we got a bit diverted there, didn't we? My name is Smith, Margaret Smith. Well, I was quite upset, as you can imagine, so I phoned up the court and said I wanted to complain, but they said that if I wanted to have my say I should turn up at South-Western at the designated time and do my bit. So I went all the way over there, right next to the Arts Centre, actually, near the Junction, you know, next to the police station but opposite that trendy café, yes, that's the one, and what a bloody farce that was.

There I stood in the silly little box in front of all these boring-looking people, wasting everybody's time talking about my rubbish. I hadn't even realised it was an offence, I said, and I was very upset about the whole incident. I was quite happy to admit it was my rubbish outside the door because Marie, my cleaner, comes every week on a Wednesday and empties all the bins into one big bag and then puts that bag outside the door. Well, it was quite funny really because, at this point, a lady barrister who was just sitting there waiting for her case to come on after mine jumped up, looking all agitated, and said that she didn't want to cut in to the proceedings in an unprofessional way, but that, technically speaking, my plea was clearly wrong as I wasn't the guilty party in this matter. No, I didn't say a word. I didn't have a clue what was going on, to be honest, so I kept my mouth shut. The clerk interrupted her and said, yes, yes, he knew all about that and he'd been just about to tell the Bench exactly the same thing. He was quite certain, therefore, that they didn't need Counsel to advise them as to the law. I know, that really made me laugh. What a bumptious old fool. Well, I call him old but he was pretty young really.

Then they just dismissed the case and sent me away, saying that was the end of the matter and I could go now. Apparently, since it wasn't me who put the bag out but Marie, it was Marie's fault. No, it was very amusing, this lady barrister then jumped up again and said that since the Learned Clerk was so well informed he certainly wouldn't need Counsel to remind him that the defendant was entitled to ask for her costs. She was great. I got into the spirit of things right away and I claimed the taxi fare from my house to the court and back again, even though I took the Number 77 bus. I made fifteen quid out of it and every penny helps.

But afterwards I was annoyed with myself because I'd never been to court before and I'd been so confused about what was going on when I got there that I hadn't taken full advantage of the opportunity to have my say. That's why I started on all this communication with Miss Flower, because it would help all of us a great deal if the rubbish vans came more than once a week. As I say, Friday is a silly day for the van to arrive, in any event, and everyone agrees, because Marjorie at number fourteen does baby-minding on Tuesdays and Wednesdays, so by Thursday there's a whole pile of rubbish out there in the street. It really attracts the dogs, who shit everywhere. Not that I mind, she can do what she likes as far as I'm concerned, but does she ever get prosecuted? No. And why is that? You're damned right. Same old story. An inspector in the local force, actually. Need we say more. No, no, far be it for me to throw the first stone. I wouldn't dream of casting aspersions but it makes you wonder, doesn't it? I mean, wouldn't you agree that it's just a little bit too coincidental to be merely coincidental?

Anyway, how're we doing for time? You couldn't possibly jog up to her office, Tina, could you? And just see if she's even there. Of course I realise how hard it is for you, especially now that your husband's left and all that, but, well, what can I say? Tina, you're an angel. I could kiss you. You're a real darling. Yes, of course, don't you worry, I won't ring off while you're gone. I'm in for the duration now, I'm holding on.

in absentia

Madeleine is pregnant, Eliza is unobtainable, Felicity is fed up. Felicity was once a member of a rock solid friendship group. Every vacation a fructiferous fortnight full of unfiltrated, filthy fun. But this year it was, apparently, not to be. The annual atlas-scouring reunion had been and gone and neither of the other girls had noticed. Times they are a-changing, she warbled tunelessly, never having completed her evening classes in singing for the tone deaf. Our lives are all moving outwards from the same epicentre but in totally different directions.

This was quite a serious reflection for someone of Felicity's good-time disposition and she almost immediately abandoned the process as a morbid and maudlin exercise. Less thinking, she thought, and more sexual intercourse. If they all want to sit around at home, having children, moping about tardy partners, watching for the telephone to ring, then let them. I do not believe in reincarnation, she said to herself, no longer having a friend available to whom she could address these words, so I will take this one chance to experience the great football match of life and I must seize all of those Premier Division balls with both hands. I will not wait for time's winged chariot to rot my stinking corpse. Although generally prosaic, Felicity had always enjoyed the Metaphysicals. The characters frequently got their knickers off in woods and fields and then died in splendidly moving ways. Or was that the Romantics? She would remember to ask Madeleine about this, she thought, on her return from her humectant holiday in Crete.

Crete, however, was dry. The weather was fine, the discos were empty. The fine-bodied waiters who had once graced the bars had moved, with the advent of the Single European Market, to northern climes, from where they sent large sums of Deutschemarks home to their loved ones and hoped not to be burned to death before they had the opportunity to spend them. Felicity realised that she was once again descending into melancholia, and, hit by an onset of polysyllabic emotions, she sank into a gloom. Mrs Spinakapoulos, the cleaner who arrived every morning to sweep the lino-covered beach-resort floor, spoke just a few potent monosyllables of English. She was exactly the kind of companion that Felicity needed. Beaming broadly, her white and red housecoat tucked into the loose elastic of the massive panty girdle which covered only some small portion of her extensive lower body, Mrs S cooed the words 'frish, frish' repeatedly and, between luscious mopping movements, shoved her pock-filled face forwards into the copy of *Hello!* which Felicity had purchased at the airport.

Felicity looked up from her coloured photos of royal ravers

and gazed out beyond Mrs S's vast and volcanically heaving bosom. She squinted through the broad shafts of mid-morning sun at the securely enclosed field directly opposite her en suite room. If you can defeat the minotaur of Crete, she thought, any one of your life's wishes will come true. She stared at a lone, imprisoned bull, pacing mournfully in the distance, and considered her numerous, unrealised desires.

The local café owner had already noticed Felicity and her licentious good looks. He willingly took her down to the field and led her to its crooked, wooden stile. But, much to his disappointment, she wished to enter alone. The field wobbled and shifted under her feet. Grassy knolls and vales sprang up unexpectedly from under the soles of her jazzy blue and silver sandals and spinnies of silver birch appeared unexpectedly from nowhere. It was the landscape of dreams, stretching downwards gently towards an impossibly lucid Mediterranean sea, and sweetened by the scent of ripening pine.

As she approached the fantastical creature she immediately discovered her mistake. On closer inspection this was no regular bull but a very individual minotaur. He was composed of one vast shopping bag made of washed grey netting, just like the ones her mother used to take to the Co-op on Saturday mornings. Felicity thought of her mother's womanly wiles and, at the moment when the minotaur suddenly charged rampantly towards her, she adroitly and astonishingly dived underneath its holey, filipanderous body and, snappily unrolling the multipurpose clingfilm which she just happened to have handy in her sarong pocket, she wrapped her arms around the bull's writhing, string-vest of a body and, grabbing it hard against her beating parts, held the machismo creature in a life or death embrace. There was a moment of tension and then the bull gave way. Buckled in half under the intense pressure of the kitchen roll, it collapsed, breathing heavily onto the mud-covered ground.

'I concede defeat,' he said, and moaned audibly about his fate. 'Today's girls are so full of power and so unpredictably dextrous with their state-of-the-art houseperson's tools.' The minotaur's face was distorted by the cellophane in which today's woman had now bound his entire twitching and convulsive body and bullishly he gasped for breath, chanting the magic slogan, 'Oh, powerful modern woman of my dreams, your wish is my command.'

Felicity said, 'I'm not really a demanding creature. I just want to see what my top scoring centre forward, Donga Doug, is doing right now. That's all I ask for. A simple fly-on-the-wall action replay of my most recent partner will suffice, since, after all, what can money do that sex can't?'

The heavily exhaling monster didn't agree with this proposition but said that it was her wish he was granting and who was he to question her rather dubious values in life? Still he was glad to see that she wasn't just an eighties' child, and this did make a change from some of the young girls who entered his field of dreams and asked for low-interest mortgage repayment schemes.

The scene changed. Felicity found that she was no longer by the ocean in Crete but standing, poised, elegant and apparently invisible, in Doug's blazingly white living-room. It was empty. She went over to the mantelpiece with its bought-in, original marble fireplace and its centrepiece – the shining framed certificate for Best Newcomer to the Field of Investigative Journalism. Next to it she saw a letter covered in the superlatively italic handwriting which, although she had never had the privilege of seeing before, she knew immediately that to be Doug's.

She walked over to the missive and picked it up. It was full of love. *Jemima,* it read, *my very own hippychick, united we stand. I know, my rock and roll baby, that you, for one, respect me wholeheartedly for what I have done and that confirmation is keeping me in the highest of spirits here in the famine zone. The years of penitence can be as nothing compared to the knowledge of your requited love. My Jem in the crown, I'm happy that you even exist in this world. I'm sad that I am not able to be with you always. Roll one for me, lover, Dougal.*

Felicity was really pissed off. Who the fuck was Jemima? She'd never read such a pile of melodramatic rubbish. It didn't even sound like Doug, and, in fact, it wasn't, since he now appeared to be called Dougal. Had she known this particular intimate but repellant detail, she would never have agreed to sleep with him. Suddenly, from nowhere, the minotaur's voice boomed into her ear. 'You may be wilier than me,' he bellowed, 'but you sure know how to waste a wish.'

She couldn't afford to stand around and waste time weeping. Felicity went over to Doug's phone. Picking it up, she began to dial the numbers of everyone she had ever known. She phoned International Directory Enquiries and asked for the number of anyone female who happened to live in Melbourne. She noticed that the phone had a Mercury compatible button but she chose not to use it and instead she had a long conversation with a woman in Auckland about the rapidly increasing appearance of ugly satellite dishes on the roofs of houses in their respective streets and the ever more rapidly decreasing value of men. She telephoned her mother who was on holiday in Cannes, her sister who was living in a hippie commune on one of the thousand islands of British Columbia and the leader of a tribe native to Papua New Guinea whom she had once read about and who sounded interesting. That should strip his assets, she thought, as the vision of Doug's flat faded away before her, melting once more into the grassy verges of Cretan fields.

The minotaur appeared before her, smiling craftily, and said, 'You don't happen to be into bestiality, do you? I know you're not the kind of virgin I normally go for, but I do rather admire a woman with the power to dominate.'

'I'm not sure,' said Felicity. 'I did once share my bed with a Siamese cat but I had an attack of hayfever halfway through the night. Still, you can't know until you try, can you? I'm the original "never say no" girl, after all, and I can always study you as a living example of sexist-generated tribal mythology, which might just help me to finish off the thesis I've been trying to complete for the last eight-and-a-half years.'

'I don't want your pity,' said the minotaur. 'I'm not just a number in a loose woman's score count. I'm not that kind of bull. I need more, much more out of a relationship. Febrifacient Felicity,' he said, 'I simply want you to love me.'

'I would find it hard to love anyone with clingfilm stuck all over his face and a vocabulary I don't understand,' said Felicity, 'but it is true that I'm attracted to you on a physical level. If both partners want the relationship to work then it will, that's what I say. So, my Taurean tank, we might as well give it a go. Be my dream-animal, you hairy beast, you, but I bags go on top because I can see from just looking at your incredible hulk of a naked body that you're going to move the earth.'

They made deep, sensitive, passionate love twice, and they even kissed. Felicity much admired the beast's lusciously hairy chest and the minotaur said it was great to do it with an experienced woman who didn't necessarily expect to be all-consumed at the end of the encounter. All the ultimate sacrifice girls did lay heavy on the stomach in the long run, he mused, and, what's more, he had been thinking about becoming a vegetarian.

Felicity was happy. She had met the creature of her dreams and, incredibly, he was heterosexual. What more could she ask for, she thought to herself, as she once again took the bull by the horns and capaciously yelled, 'yes.'

joking apart

With his wife Rebecca, Jerry Joneth celebrates the end of his three-month battle against injustice.

Jerry Joneth, whom we have all heard so much about over these last few weeks since his recent court case, is a swinger.

In this exclusive interview in which Jerry and Rebecca Joneth show us around their gorgeous home somewhere in West London, we start by printing this photo of the living-room where, he tells us, he stores his private collection of over two hundred and fifty crotch-wrenching seventies tunes. Here you see another picture of him standing poised by his alphabetically filed record rack, practising his hip gyrations to the super cool sounds of one of his all-time favourite bands, KC and the Sunshine Band. He has, he tells us, one of the most important private collections of coloured vinyl 12″ discs in Britain today.

'And is that how you will spend the unbelievably massive, six-figure damages that you were awarded in the High Court this week?' we ask him as he shows us into his bathroom, looks into his silver-plated, pull-out shaving mirror and slicks back his hair. 'You're a nice-looking boy, Jimbo,' we tell him, as he reaches jauntily for the hair gel, 'we all think you're one cotton-picking cute little lad.'

That is, he tells our reporter, why he is so glad to be rich. It's not the material goods that matter to him, that's certainly not why he pursued this libel action with such vigour. It's being able to afford the favours of people to whom he is sexually attracted.

'And, let's face it, you dog,' he says in his incomparably witty and laconic way whilst kissing his lickerous reflection in the squeaky clean mirror before him, 'you're attracted to almost anyone and ain't that the truth. Joking apart,' he concludes, pulling himself smartly together for this rather touching composition with his lovely wife, Rebecca, 'it's the principle of the thing that motivated me. Rebecca and I were both put through much unnecessary hardship because of this whole scandal, which was an utter, utter disgrace in every way and a violation of my sanctified privacy rights as an upstanding citizen and member of the community. I am now, with the help and encouragement of just a fraction of the good people who have supported me throughout my action, thinking of standing for parliament, and that is the only reason, of course, that I agreed to do this interview today. I feel so strongly about the great injustice that I have suffered that my greatest aim in life now is to put a private member's bill through parliament and, in some small way, add my personal contribution, to the curbing of some of the worst excesses of the press. And Rebecca thinks so too.

'Not that I am in any way in favour of censorship. Far from it. I consider myself to be a liberal in every way. But, as I'm sure all right-thinking people would agree, there have to be limits, boundaries beyond which the money-grabbing exploiters of what was once called Fleet Street cannot cross.' Jerry knits his brow at this time and we take this thoughtful shot of him in his aluminium-coated Poggenpohl kitchen as his wife pours us all some jasmine tea.

'And how do you feel about your husband's new career?' we ask the fragrant Rebecca, who, we must say, really does look radiant in her Chinese silk dress with its bright blue petit point embroidery and its appliquéed red lion motif.

She tells us that she will support her husband in every way possible. It has been a difficult year for both of them but her devotion to him has never once wavered and the welcome encouragement she has received from all their many supporters, both at home and abroad, has sustained her and her husband through these troubled times. She would like to extend a grateful thank you, however, to all of the many people without whose selfless help she doesn't know how she would have coped.

Rebecca looks tearful at this point and her husband walks over and holds her hand. He is, quite clearly, devoted to her and how anyone could have thought otherwise is certainly beyond all of us. He produces a handkerchief and wipes away her tears. She smiles up at him and blushes modestly. It is a touching scene, indeed, and our photographer now takes the charming domestic portrait that you see in the bottom left-hand corner of this page, along with an inset photo of the ring that Jerry gave Rebecca last week on the public reconfirmation of their wedding vows which they celebrated in the beautiful and ancient St Bride's Church.

'And are there any plans for little Joneths?' we ask the happy couple. Rebecca is bashful and says that, naturally, they have many, many other things to achieve before they can consider taking such a serious and responsible step in life, but that they love one another a great deal and it was something they were both very much looking forward to when the time was right.

Here is a photo of Rebecca sitting on their splendid four-poster bed. She tells us that she bought the Egyptian linen duvet cover at Heal's and that she would very much recommend it to other women with skin as sensitive as hers. It is entirely non-allergenic, just like the make-up range she uses and which you see displayed here, in her environmentally sound changing room.

The couple now take us into the study. Jerry shows us his fax machine and stresses the importance of up-to-the-minute communication networks. He turns out to be an expert on modem technology and gives us a highly proficient demonstration then and there. Rebecca tells us, blushingly, that perhaps this room will have another function one day, but that, of course, only time will tell. Jerry says, yes, they have been thinking about installing a pool table or a bar skittles set, but he doesn't think that there is quite enough room to get a decent swing action going. Rebecca wipes a mote of dust from the VDU screen and blushes again.

We find their domestic badinage utterly charming.

And now the Joneths treat us to a special dinner they have prepared entirely for our benefit. Here is a photo of the astonishing way in which they have laid out the table with an exquisite eye for the aesthetics of eating. The first course consists of a hollowed-out pumpkin containing a soup of their own devising which they have somehow managed to dye a full, rich, golden colour. Floating gracefully on the top, we see a handful of remarkable silver-coloured croutons. It's just a little something she prepared earlier, explains Rebecca. We don't think so! We provide the recipe for this superbly flavoured dish on page 56 and we are sure that you will enjoy it quite as much as we did.

Rebecca says that she doesn't need to watch her weight. She is naturally petite. Her only advice to the rest of us, less fortunate, ladies, is that she doesn't eat meat and she finds this to be no problem at all. Of course, it's more work to rustle up a quiche than to grill a simple steak but Jerry and Rebecca very much enjoy the simple things in life. For the main course, they serve us with the perfect omelette aux fines herbes. It is a joy. Rebecca shrugs when we tell her that we have always considered an omelette one of the most difficult creations in any chef's repertoire. 'It's just a question of following the recipe,' she tells us. 'I find Julia Child's book particularly helpful where eggs are concerned.'

The pudding is the lightest of lemon soufflés. At the end of the meal, we enjoy that perfect state of repletion without overindulgence in which we all strive to leave our guests. What a superb house! What a superb repast! What a superb couple! Let us congratulate them on their recent victory in the courts and let us all hope for more good news from them both in the near future. Take note, potential electors, we are all relying on your good taste and judgement to return Jerry Joneth to the well-deserved but challenging new position. Judging by his past performance, we are sure that he will enjoy it immensely. People of Britain, the choice is yours.

knackered

Eliza was overcome by unidentified flying emotions, a state of affairs which had taken her very much by surprise. Whenever her friend Madeleine droned on about the benefits of nuptial bliss, Eliza had listened with a keen sororial interest but had always remained utterly mystified by the feelings that her friend was attempting to portray. The two women enjoyed one another's company immensely and loved each other almost without condition, yet, despite all this abundant companionship, Madeleine's words often had no meaning for Eliza.

Intellectually, she could understand what Madeleine's vocabulary was deemed to label but she had no conception of the emotional content that it might contain.

In Eliza's world view, men had always been a Brighton Pier experience. You went on an excursion; you ate some candy floss; it made a mess all over your face; you probably lost some money on the fruit machines but, what the hell, at the end of the day you were bound to be sick all over the car upholstery so you might as well just enjoy it while it lasted. Fuck them first, get to know them later, that was the motto of the fine-featured Felicity, and one that she and Eliza had always tried to live down to.

Relationships are bound to go wrong, Felicity told her, eventually you'll come to realise that Mr Miracle is either boring or a treacherous brute and then he'll forget to telephone. You'll spend all of your time worrying about what he's feeling and how he relates to you and you'll begin to lose sight of what should be the key issue which is how you feel about him. In the end it's bound to be a total waste of the emotional and creative energy that you should be spending on yourself, so, my old and dearest friend, the answer is to cut out the cancer and make love to the skeleton. What's more, you burn off as many calories in one session as you do in a six-mile jog, so, the way I see it, you're killing two birds with one fuck.

Men tended to be terrified of Felicity's sexual accomplishments. They considered her manipulative and hard, which she wasn't. Neither was she the bitter and twisted former victim, as the slightly patronising Madeleine tended to think. Eliza felt she understood Felicity better, since she considered herself to be positioned somewhere in the sexual middle ground between the chaste and the promiscuous.

Generally, when Felicity started spouting her 'philosophy of the physical', as she liked to call it, Eliza would take a pragmatic approach. It was perfectly acceptable to be such a dilettante with other people's emotions when you were as physically attractive as Felicity with her almond eyes and her legs that didn't touch at the thighs. Felicity could be as emotionally temporary as she liked, since there would always be an endless wellspring of men queuing up to supply fodder for her combine harvester of a sexual appetite. Eliza did know that this was an irrelevance but couldn't stop herself thinking that she herself would never be in such a fortunate position.

She did fully appreciate, however, that Felicity was not conscious of dealing with any of her boyfriends in anything less than an entirely genuine way and Eliza, indeed, very much admired Felicity's robustness and self-containment. If you want to fuck, jump on his dick, said Felicity, who, Eliza felt, must be sub-consciously aware that very few men would be confident enough of their own sexuality to jump on Felicity's abounding delights. Eliza, though not disapproving, knew that she was different. Her friend's conduct seemed too technical to Eliza, as if Felicity was attempting to gain the Brownies' silver medal in performance skills. She wasn't judgemental but she recognised that she was too emotional ever to be able to behave in as sexually dispassionate a fashion as Felicity.

But she never discussed this thorny knot with either of her two intimates, apart from in the most general and abstract of terms. They could all be friends and would continue to coexist quite happily knowing that this diversity of world views made their friendship more stimulating and educative but all three were constantly aware that their emotional responses to life could only ever be divided, different and utterly separate. All three considered that their particular emotional response was the right one but not that the other women's were wrong. All three knew that there were no words with which one could adequately discuss this fragile emotional equilibrium without causing its collapse. They simply chose to love one another to the best of their abilities and hoped, in the most generous of ways, never to be the one to disturb the finely tuned balance.

At Madeleine's wedding to Paul, a man whom Felicity and Eliza both tolerated but despised, Eliza was the single, unblushing bridesmaid who deliberately dropped the bouquet.

She found the life that Madeleine had chosen for herself to be repellent and destructively conventional. Eliza's own life was more modern, more glamorous and more challenging. But, looking at the bride, who was smiling away at the centre of the action and having the time of her life, Eliza felt an intense and inexplicable envy of an existence that she in no way desired for herself.

Felicity, who was making the most of the opportunity to charm the rather trendy, if prematurely balding, young priest, discovered that he was in a punk-rock-reggae-dub band. Much to his delight she promised to go and listen to him playing the bass guitar at his next gig, while also managing to get across the information that she had always found the dog collar a particularly arousing item of clothing. The ceremony left her personally untouched. Its function was entirely alien and she considered the whole value system that it entailed to be a pile of retrogressive bollocks. Eliza wished that she could be so indifferent. She knew that she was being unkind and petty but at the time she could only feel that she wanted to lash out at Madeleine's incomprehensible and very public moment of happiness.

Scoop, the best man and Paul's oldest mate, was gorgeous. He had curly, jet black hair and big, brown eyes and, even in a morning suit, he closely resembled Jesus. Eliza had always admired self-sacrifice.

'Scoop,' she said, as she wandered over to a position just opposite his most prominent muscle group, 'I can't help myself, I just had to come over here and tell you that you're by far the best-looking man in this aisle.'

'You're not too bad yourself, sunshine,' he replied as he pinched her right buttock quite forcefully. Normally this would have motivated Eliza to knee him in the balls, but on this occasion she felt an unplundered malicious urge to ruin Madeleine's afternoon.

Eliza and Scoop pretended that they had forgotten some essential ceremonial item in the cemetery and exited via a mediaeval threshold to pursue their mutual enquiries.

Subsequently, Eliza cried all the way through the two-thirds of the service that she didn't miss and Madeleine's mother approached her at the reception and told her that she knew exactly how Eliza felt. It was like becoming an adult and losing your innocence forever all in forty-five minutes, she said. Eliza, in total sincerity, agreed. The whole afternoon was about as close as she had ever come to a spiritual experience, although she never heard from Scoop again.

Perhaps it was best that way, she told Felicity later, since it meant that Madeleine, who would undoubtedly be pissed off, was less likely to find out about the escapade. But Felicity, who had no agenda of her own and simply thought that it was a cracking good story, had by this time already told Madeleine, who had chosen to rise way above such single women's considerations. She certainly wasn't going to let it ruin her memories of the big day. It was, for her, both too trivial to mention, since it would then take on a significance it did not deserve, and at the same time too significant to discuss, since its implications for both women ran far deeper than either would choose to admit. Madeleine realised that she would never be able to mention the incident again. Eliza, feeling unaccountably guilty, thought that she ought. At regular intervals she would try to bring the subject up and would joke about having a long session in which they would both air their mutual, secret grievances once and for all and then be able to forget them forever. Madeleine had smiled sympathetically and nodded. You can forgive, she knew, but you can never forget.

Felicity was never prone to such mires of introspection. Eliza felt she had been disproportionately interested in the variety of sexual positions that one could sustain on a gravestone and in whether the sheer solidity of the cold, hard stone had added a certain *je ne sais quoi* to the conjunction. In order to please Felicity, Eliza had discussed this point at great length and had thus trivialised an act which had been really quite significant. The two women drank a bottle of vodka with some garlic olives and fun-filled Felicity literally pissed herself laughing, while Eliza drew some sketchy but graphic diagrams and transformed the whole event into one of Felicity's sexually liberated, ultimately controlled, modern woman's fictions. In Eliza's mind the story became a comic one and, later, she could remember it in no other terms. She wheeled it out regularly at the dinner parties of people about whose moral approbation she did not care. They always considered it a very saucy tale indeed.

Years later when Madeleine was still extolling the virtues of marital harmony and Felicity was knocking up her score-card in a particularly Grand National way, Eliza, searching for interval refreshments at the Barbican, quite by chance bumped into a man who had once had a massive thing about a mutual university friend. Neither of them saw this girl much any more and they both had a laugh about the dreadful people one would have ended up marrying were there still a social understanding that you should hitch up permanently with the person with whom you happened to be making love at the time you graduated from university. Rather enchantingly, Stanley then queued up for Eliza in the theatre foyer while she went to the toilet and by the time she returned, now wearing lipstick, he had bought her a high-quality strawberry ice cream. She remarked upon this and asked how he could possibly have known that it was her favourite flavour. He replied that he hadn't known, it was just a stroke of luck, there was nothing significant about it. He liked strawberry also. They had a short chat about the fact that fruits of the forest always appear in sorbet but never in ice cream, and after this Stan returned to his friends who all looked as if they were having a much better time than Eliza. On Eliza's mentioning her penchant for strawberry ice cream to her date for the evening, Gus was inspired, just a little later, to treat her to an outrageously erotic evening in the kitchen when they got home. Eliza saved the empty tub as a memento and considered the whole event an all-round success.

A few weeks later, as Eliza was sitting around at home considering whether her new anagram entry for the *Time Out* Lonelyhearts advert was intellectually attractive or merely reprehensibly pretentious, Stan from the theatre trip rang quite out of the blue. Having managed to find her number in some way that was too boring to relate, he just wondered, well, how she was getting on really. She was fine, she said, doodling aimlessly on a postcard of Bonnard's wife in the bath. Get on with it, she thought. You wouldn't have rung if you didn't want to invite me out to dinner so just go ahead and invite me. Stan serpentined in a terribly transparent way around a variety of not uninteresting topics until Eliza could bear it no more and put him out of his misery.

'So when am I going to see you?' she asked, and he smiled audibly and took heart.

Dinner, over a fortnight later since she was a busy girl, was unexceptional. They chatted about their desert island books in a perfectly undynamic way. He smiled a lot and continually leaned forward earnestly to tell her how great it was to see her after all these years. She couldn't respond to this motion in any constructive way since she didn't remember him from their former acquaintance. Still, he was pretty funny, he flattered her in the right places and then he offered to pay for the meal. She didn't want to let him, although she knew that Felicity would rebuke her for this later, and they almost got into a fight about the bill. She conceded defeat in a most graceful way and kissed him a 'thank you' on the back of his neck as they rose to leave. He blushed to the roots of his cautious being and absolutely insisted on giving her a lift home. She thought this rather sweet. He was clearly kind and relatively interesting, but there was something about his prominent chin and gangly body that disturbed her and she didn't want to prolong his anxiety in any way.

So the upshot was that she didn't invite him in to look at her etchings. He took what could only be considered as total rejection in good spirits and, looking disappointed but optimistic, waved enthusiastically through the car window and honked on his horn several times as he drove away up her street. She waved back limply and promptly lost his number.

Many weeks later on her return from her annual holiday with the girls, Eliza was sitting by herself at home, avidly reading every article she could find about Jerry's exposure as a bisexual rubber fetishist, and his humiliating but financially lucrative libel action. There were some fluorescent blue descriptions of impossibly Houdini-like positions in the papers and a couple of terrifically voyeuristic photos. Jerry's wife, Rebecca, appeared from time to time on the front pages, looking tearful but virulently fragrant and always unimpeachably virginal. Good for her, said Felicity, but I bet they don't give the money to charity.

Eliza was keen to ring Jerry and offer herself as a charitable cause since he was proving to be suave, articulate and highly moral in the witness box. But so too was the rewardingly chaste Rebecca, about whom Eliza had known nothing. In any case, the number that Jerry had given her, remained, unsurprisingly, unobtainable. Eliza assumed that she was on the bottom of Jerry's list of concerns. The extra-marital context itself was not a problem for her. She considered that if Rebecca was prepared to put up with this philandering, then that was surely Rebecca's own problem, but she was only too familiar with the rules of the dating game and knew that to try and persuade someone that they are attracted to you is about as self-defeatingly unattractive as it is possible to be. So she just let sleeping dicks lie and read, at great length, about the shockingly painful-sounding nipple mutilation and mused on what might have been.

And then the phone rang.

'Who?' she said, still in some distant, erotic torture chamber of her own creation. 'Oh yes, of course, Stan, yes, and how are you?'

Stan, rather hesitantly, asked her what kind of music she liked. Oh anything, she said, knowing full well where this conversation would lead but not being able to guess off the top of her head what he might have considered her taste in music to be. Shostakovich, he said. He knew it was a bit unusual and that some people felt it was gloomy with no good tunes but he liked the guy and he thought that she would too. And the cellist was rather a snazzy performer. Eliza tried to remember the last time she had heard someone use the word 'snazzy'. She said it sounded interesting.

She was very glad that Stan had thought of her while she'd been lying around on her multi-coloured Indian cushions working herself up into a state of unprecedented gloom. She decided that he was a nice fellow and that she liked him. Shostakovich, she said, was one of her very favourites, just like strawberry ice cream. On this second date, however, he was far less willing to expose his vulnerabilities. He arranged to meet at the concert shortly before it started; he said nothing about dinner afterwards and he mentioned the nearest tube.

Despite herself, Eliza began to feel anxious. Given her own feelings of disinterest, she absurdly started to consider the possibility that he didn't fancy her at all. He just happened to have a spare ticket available and he had rung up everyone he knew in order that it should not go to waste. She realised she was being ridiculous. But on the Shostakovich evening she made a special effort when she got dressed and she changed her clothes three times, losing confidence continually and deciding that she looked awful in just about everything she owned. She phoned Madeleine to discuss this conundrum but Madeleine launched into the woes of morning sickness and Eliza conceded that this was a considerably more important development in their lives than a date with a weedy, timorous, dried raisin of a fellow, so she shut up. But she carried on thinking about Stan.

He was great. He was funny and attentive and kind. He still looked like a piece of dried fruit but Eliza ceased to notice. She was quite, quite charmed by the sheer range of his conversation. He was acutely interested in the anthropology of menstrual ritual and not in the least embarrassed to discuss it with her. She was flattered by his interest and exhilarated by his contributions to the argument. She couldn't believe that she had not spotted all this on their earlier date. She could have kicked herself for the humbling way in which she had treated him but sensed that he would be generous-spirited enough to give her a second chance. She astonished herself.

At the end of the concert he said goodnight and didn't try to kiss her. She stared at him in horror but he had already gone. She felt unjustifiably upset by this but knew that it was merely frustrated pride. It wasn't as if she could ever have sex with a dehydrated prune, after all. She went home feeling a little low. She couldn't sleep. She tossed and turned. She phoned Felicity.

'Oh for God's sake,' said Felicity, 'he's obviously shy. Take him out for the day, come back late to his place, get your kit off and Bob's your uncle. You're laughing.'

Eliza asked her other oracle. Madeleine also agreed that it was obviously not an attraction problem since it was he who had invited her in the first place. 'But the guy needs time,' she said, 'he needs to feel his way cautiously to a position of sexual confidence. He's probably a sensitive soul. Give him time.'

'Sod that,' said Felicity, 'if you don't do it soon, it will never happen. You must know that. And no man is going to say "no". The very idea is laughable, and you're a lovely gorgeous girl, and you just remember to bear that in mind.'

Madeleine said, 'But ask yourself, why? Why are you doing this? Only because your pride is piqued and he has shown no interest in you. Ask yourself, at all times, do you really want this? You are number one. Remember that.'

'Of course,' said Felicity, 'no one could doubt that. And what the fuck is number one going to get out of it, if she's not going to get a fuck out of it. Ay,' she added, 'there's the rub,' feeling rather pleased with her linguistic dexterity.

Eliza sat at home, composing a new anagram. She certainly wasn't going to give up on her other options in favour of a potential encounter with a bowl of dried fruit. And then the telephone rang.

'Of course,' she said, jumping up and spilling peppermint tea all over her *Time Out*. Of course she would love to. She was thrilled. She was so happy. She was worried that she had begun to suffer from irrational feelings about a morsel of prune and she wanted to know what this might mean.

'Remember to wear your best knickers,' said Felicity. 'All that kind of thing is very important on a first sexual encounter. And no woolly tights or body stockings that are hard to remove.'

'Try and build up his confidence,' said Madeleine. 'He's obviously a nice boy, bit shy. Wait for him to make the pass or you'll frighten him off.'

'You'll never get anywhere if you wait,' was Felicity's final contribution to the debate. 'Just remember, the simple adage, "fuck, fuck, fuck". That's very important.'

Eliza decided on black lace but non-frilly underwear and felt nervous. She had already lost sight of what she herself wanted. She felt sensitive and highly strung. But did she even fancy him? Was this a relevant question? She looked in the mirror, told herself that she was pretty and waited for the buzzer to sound.

He was punctual. His car was not smart. They had a routings discussion. M25, he posited, and then cut across to the M4.

'Perhaps not,' she said, 'because there have been a lot of roadworks on the Westway of late.'

'Ah yes,' he said, 'but we are catching the contraflow.'

'Nice word,' said Eliza, 'but what do you mean by that exactly?'

'It's an opposite,' he said. 'We're going in the alternative direction to the rest of the populace, don't you agree?'

'I agree,' she said, smiling, 'wholeheartedly. Then you choose the route, and you take the consequent responsibility for your actions.'

Stan smiled and, plumping for his own personal routing option after all, leaned over in the car and touched the back of her hand. Eliza felt really good.

Several hours later, picnicking on the slip road of an unmoving M25, and, in the middle of a joke about words beginning with the letter 'Q' but not containing a 'U', Stan suddenly said, 'So how do you feel about me?'

Eliza was startled. She was having a great day. They had caught the flow, the contraflow, the rush hour and the road-works but she was still having a fabulous time. Her second-best knickers, she was sure, were by now quite moist, but she didn't wish to ruin a great day. Although it had been inevitable, now that the question had arrived it was too soon.

'I think you're great,' she said.

'But you don't find me physically attractive.'

'That's kind of irrelevant,' she considered thoughtfully, 'and anyway, it's not true.'

'I think you're lovely and gorgeous and generous and clever and cultured,' said Stan,

'This is great,' she said. 'Do carry on.'

'And that's why I don't want to have sex with you.'

'I wish you hadn't carried on.'

Eliza was silent and headed back to the car. She was confused. Fuck, fuck, fuck, she thought, and she wasn't talking about the philosophy of the physical. She wished she had a cell-phone. This scenario was new to her and she needed some advice.

'Say something,' said Stan. 'Talk to me.'

'I don't know what to say,' said Eliza, 'since I don't wish to embarrass myself but personally I was aiming for the less talk, more action option. That's what normally happens when you get on well with someone of the opposite sex.'

'Of course I care about you immensely,' said Stan. 'How can you even doubt that?'

'Well, then what's your problem, sweetheart?' said Eliza. 'Are you trying to tell me you've got some sexual hang-up, then? You're impotent, you're married, you're gay?'

'I don't have a problem,' said Stan, just a touch defensively, as Eliza looked around the car for stickers of the Pope at prayer. 'But I do feel that we have a special understanding. If I fucked you – I mean, if we fucked each other, of course – it would ruin everything. You are too precious to me to destroy what is undoubtedly going to be a beautiful friendship.'

'Fucking hell,' said Eliza, 'we're not characters in *Casablanca*, for God's sake. I have to think that you're desperately sexually insecure or that you don't fancy me. Either way, that's your problem, Stan, but I can only feel personally insulted and rejected by what you are saying. So you've already destroyed any potential friendship we might have had by asking the question.'

Stan was silent.

'I don't want you to feel rejected,' he said as they approached the Junction 15/4B interchange. 'I'm not rejecting you.'

'This is stupid,' said Eliza, 'and you've just gone and ruined the whole day.'

Stan looked miserable.

Sensitive men, thought Eliza. Who needs them?

letter of love

My darling Jemima

Finally I find myself frying in the famine fields. Frankly, it's no fun. But the fates have fixed my fortunes forever and the financial fiasco which led to my editor both flattering my fine prose and flushing me from my fifth floor filing cabinet now finalises itself with me, in fuming fugitivism, somewhere in flea-ridden Africa. I am floundering, fumbling, falling without your fond and feeling face beside my femur.

But the name shall not pass. Fever may rack my brow, frost may flush its freezing way throughout my fingers, but finer feelings will never allow Fleet Street's greatest secret to pass from my fragile lips. It is flailed fast upon my heart. As I have told only you, my fondling, the initial letter of the source of my information is all that I will ever reveal of the roots of my frightful facts. The 'F' word will remain forever a secret forged furiously into my flesh. We may have lost the libel action but we shall never lose our principles. For some the sacrifice is great. For me, it is your fantastic figure.

My full moon, my forceps, my Fomalhaut (you might have to look that one up), I'm sitting here on my footstool, thinking of you. It's not nearly as exciting as I thought it would be out here on the frontline with only the OED for company. I will spend my free time feverishly finalising fan mail to you and this far-sighted fixation will fix you firmly to my failing spirits. For us 'F' will always symbolise the letter of love, since it is the 'F' word which divides us, seemingly, forever.

Flamingly

Doug

My dearest Doug

I miss you a lot, too, and I think that I understand what you're getting at but could we, perhaps, try it out with a slightly easier letter? I'm finding the 'F' word rather hard-going and I think it might facilitate my flow if we tried one of the letters that only gets one point in Scrabble. I'm sending you a special, magnetised travel set along with this note so that you'll have something to do with all your spare time and you'll be able to see what I mean.

Faint-heartedly

Jemima

P.S. I read your article on guerrilla warfare and I do realise that you've been very vulnerable about your writing skills since the day you were humiliatingly transferred to an obscure part of Africa. I certainly wouldn't wish to cramp your flow in any way, but I have to say, in all honesty, that I did find your style just a little bit fulsome. Tone it down a bit, sweetheart, or I will continue to suffer, on reading your prose, from an unpleasant sense of formication (you might have to look that one up).

My darling Ms Jarvis

Please.

Flakiness was never one of your former foibles. Frankness perhaps, lack of fellow-feeling sometimes, flatulence frequently, but flakiness, my love, I forecast more from my fabulous flying fish.

So give it another go.

By the way I met quite an interesting guy. He's the correspondent for one of the other dailies and we've been hanging out together and bonding quite a lot. He's been here for a while already and he's built up some great contacts in the revolutionary movement which we're going to work on together. The newspaper says it wants some more quirky human interest stories, not too many starving children, no politics. So we're going to try and chase up an idea about a tribe on a diet of worms (I thought that had a certain ring to it which I know that you, my love, will appreciate) and, maybe, we'll bounce some ideas off each other and write a few features on a day in the life of a mud hut, that kind of thing. Fill me in with some feedback, please, but constructively this time. I miss you terribly and am very lonely.

Frustratedly

Doug

Dear Doug

I think the sun must be going to your head. 'Diet of Worms' is, quite frankly, frightful. And is your friend good-looking?

Yours

Jemima

Dear Jemima,

That was unnecessarily cruel. So, okay, we'll forget about the 'F' word for the minute. I have no wish to dwell on the unobtainable and the heat is really getting to me. I can quite see that, perhaps, it's not the most appropriate of letters on which to dwell at the present time.

Did I ever tell you about my mate, Fred? The other day I was thinking about him and the time the two of us hired a villa in Apulia. One sultry afternoon, there was a sort of fête in the piazza and Fred took me down to the square where one of the local girls led me by the hand to the dance area, in which we gave a magnificently accomplished display of the Lambada during most of which she rubbed her pubescent groin vigorously into mine. Then her fifteen-year-old beau approached us at a rapid pace and threatened to punch my lights out for trying to steal his bird. As you know, I don't speak Italian but it was bloody obvious what he meant so me and Fred legged it back to the villa and hid for hours. That was when he gave me the nickname Spunky Tosser and it stuck for years. I never mentioned it to you before because I didn't think you'd like it very much.

I was thinking about all this just the other day, when me and Bill went to this tribal wedding in the local village. Every woman over the age of nine was carrying a baby in swaddling tied firmly to their protruding stomachs and sucking at their massive, dangling, milkless breasts. Me and Bill were left to dance with the seven-year-olds, most of whose faces already seemed aeons older than yours, you'll be pleased to hear.

I think perhaps that all this solitude is making

me introspective. I couldn't remember how to do the Lambada and we got paralytically drunk and collapsed into a flea-bitten heap on the dust-ridden floor. There isn't much else to do, really. I've already tried the diet of worms.

Yours in maudlin mood

Doug

Dear Original Spunky Tosser

This frog-march to foreign climes will obviously forge your formation both as a freelance and as a fellow.

Frothing for further footage

Your fractured friend

moment of truth

'I am in a state of severe discombobulation,' said Eliza, who had had a traumatic week and was now boring us stupid with it, 'and I feel fucking miserable.

'I don't want to go on about it,' she began again.

'So shut up,' we told her. ' For goodness sake, what has come over you? You're number one, remember. You're a gorgeous, lovely, intelligent girl.'

'That's what Stan said,' mumbled Eliza, 'and he still didn't want to fuck me.'

Eliza was being absurd. She can bore me senseless for all I care, she's one of my oldest friends and I love her dearly, and I'll simply carry on listening to all her senseless lovelife drivel, but, really, this was just plain stupid. I didn't know the guy from Adam but he'd obviously got some sexual problem, since that's what it all boils down to in the end, and, even if it was not sexual, it was still his problem if he didn't want to get physical with my special, wonderful friend. So why the hell was she the one to be getting upset? But that's always the way it goes, of course, and exactly why I choose never to get involved. It's simply a question of self-control.

I was drinking my third mug of tea and Eliza was still crapping on about this divvy guy Stan, who clearly wasn't remotely interested in her, which was exactly why she was getting so upset. I'd never even heard of the guy before last week. Well, this could hardly be love, could it? But now that she thought she'd been rejected, the one thing that she wanted most in the whole world was to feel desired by the person who'd just rejected her. What a pile of shit. I give up on her. She is utterly hopeless.

Then Paul, Madeleine's husband, went over to a kitchen drawer to retrieve a bulbous lump of old, brown Plasticine and brought it back to the three of us, depositing it dramatically on the dining-room table. He stuck a pin in the lump and placed a mirror opposite the pin and started walking, all stooped over and Quasimodo-like, from side to side, staring hard at the reflection.

'What the fuck are you playing at?' I said. I fully accept that I am intolerant of Paul, and not merely because he is our friend Madeleine's husband.

'I am attempting to make Eliza feel better,' said Paul, squinting hard and bending over even further. 'I am setting up an experiment which will demonstrate to you all an important astronomical proposition.'

I wasn't very hopeful that this would succeed in lifting Eliza's spirits. It is a long time since I have allowed myself to sink into a depression about a man and I can only dimly recall the sensation, but I know that it is an intense one and I did not think that a grubby piece of Day-glo would save the day. Still, Paul is a simple soul and he means well.

Madeleine, her stomach held before her like a vast hot air balloon, stood behind Eliza, who was the only one sitting at the table, since the experiment had been set up on her behalf, and Madeleine, in imitation of her husband (who believe me is not worth imitating), stared into the glass.

'What are we supposed to be looking for, my love?' she asked. Inexplicably, she thinks he's clever.

Eliza pulled her face to one side and tried hard not to laugh. I started laughing as well. Paul was such a hopelessly comic character, hopping around, relumping the Plasticine, shifting the mirror. We could tell that, just like everything else in Paul's life, he would try so very hard but this experiment would only ever achieve a beta plus for effort.

'What are you doing, Paul?' I asked as I caught sight of Eliza's pain-racked face in the mirror. 'Are you winning?'

'I am afraid that I cannot make it work,' he said, 'but I can explain to you all what's supposed to happen. The thing is that Eliza is upset, right, because this guy doesn't fancy her.'

'It's not as simple as that,' said Eliza, adolescently.

'Well, whatever,' said Paul, 'the point is that you're upset. Now that's your point of view from where you're sitting. So you look into this mirror and you see the reflection of the needle, right? And the reflection isn't directly opposite the subject needle, is it? And if you walk around the edge of the table like this,' he explained, skipping forwards gauchely and tripping on Eliza's discarded shoe, 'you will notice that, as you move, the needle's reflection will apparently move also.'

'So?' said Eliza, stony-faced.

'Well, that's it, really. That's the experiment. It's a visual demonstration of the concept of parallax. The image of the needle appears differently from wherever you look, even though the actual needle will always remain in the same place. The implication of this theory is that two people could never be standing in exactly the same spot at the same time, so two people could never perceive the given subject in exactly the same way.'

'That's great, Paul,' I said, 'that's the most interesting thing you've ever told me.'

'Felicity,' he said, 'thank you for the generosity of spirit which you always show in my regard. I shall now spend the rest of the afternoon bathing in your opprobrium.'

'Approbration, darling, you mean approbration,' cut in Madeleine, 'and you seem to have forgotten what happened on the evening that you wheeled this experiment out at my mother's.' Madeleine can afford to be much, much more cutting to Paul than either Eliza or I. She is married to the guy.

'The point is,' she continued, 'that on one of the numerous other occasions on which Paul has demonstrated his favourite dinner party trick – which may or may not have been at my mother's but it doesn't matter – on that occasion, one of the other guests explained to us that if you put the Plasticine in exactly the right position and the needle in precisely the right place, then you may just be able to locate a semi-mystical position called the point of no parallax and then, magically, the reflection will appear in the mirror at a position directly opposite the subject needle. It's a very difficult spot to find and, on the evening in question, we didn't succeed. Now Paul's been practising for weeks and he hasn't been able to get it right, either. But it does, theoretically, exist, and that's the point.'

What point? I thought. I didn't get it.

'None of this makes me feel in the remotest way more cheerful,' said Eliza, 'but it is fascinating. What do you suppose this elusive moment of truth would represent, then? And I'm warning you, now, that I'm only interested if it means I'd discover that he wants to fuck me after all.'

'That's hilarious,' I said. 'As far as I can make out, this is supposed to be a grandiose concept which will lead you to rise above your petty despondencies and make you realise that you need to change your subjective attitude and ignore the object completely.'

'I think you'll find it's the other way round,' said Paul, 'if you think about it.'

'Well, whatever,' I said, constantly surprised at how jerkish he can be.

'I would like to think,' said Paul, 'that it has a certain something to say for the current state of the Labour party.'

'What!' we all hooted in derisory laughter as he explained, in all earnestness, that the very existence of such a point implied a notion of objective truth which, as we all know, was the antipathy of all good socialist thought.

'Christ Almighty,' I said, 'what a pretentious git you are.'

'So if you're so bloody clever,' said Paul, 'you tell me what it might mean then.'

'Fuck knows,' I said. 'I'm not interested in that kind of thing. I'm more of an Arsenal girl myself.'

'I've been thinking about it for a few weeks now,' posited Madeleine, 'and I think it might be a religious experience. You know, spiritual union, that kind of thing, the revelation of God moment. Alternatively, it might be a moment at which you and your beloved, for just a split second, see the universe in exactly the same way, in perfect harmony of thought. Like, maybe, when you give birth or something. I know that's a bit sentimental but I'd like to think that might be it.'

'Crap,' said Eliza. 'It's impossible. I feel like shit and that's my subjective truth and that's the only truth that's valid for me. So you can all shut up and pass me the hankies and, Paul, I think you should now take the needle out of the Plasticine and use it to sew on the button which has been absent from a crucial position on your trousers for the last forty-five minutes.'

God, I love Eliza. She's just great.

naked truths

Arnold ran his own company, flushing out viruses for large corporate concerns. Margaret worked for a publisher, but not on the editorial side, as she told the creatively inclined friends of Arnold who enquired after her welfare at soirées. 'Oh no,' she would say, 'that's not really my thing. I'm more of a contracts woman. I set percentages. When Arnold's business does a little bit better I'd like to give up straightaway and have another daughter. Not a son, though, they're a bit dull when they grow up, don't you think? And, of course, we'd like to buy a house of our own somewhere central. We're not in a strong position at the moment because Arnold hasn't actually got any orders yet but he is very hopeful, aren't you, sweetheart? He's got exclusive rights, you know; it's a terrific business idea.'

Arnold looked resigned to his state of depression and stuck his face deep into his can of beer.

'I tease him mercilessly,' continued Margaret, 'but I just love him to death.'

Just lately Margaret had been worrying about their mutual rubbish. Sometimes Arnold took it in the car to the recycling centre, which their daughter very much enjoyed. There were tips marked 'green', 'clear' and 'plastic' and large men in overalls shifting corrugated metal. Margaret let Arnold take Tina by himself because Margaret found it all a little unpleasant and Arnold said that there was no point collecting the newspapers any more because the powers that be already had enough used print to last till the end of the century. Margaret took his word about that kind of thing because he worked in Science while she pursued the Arts. But, just lately, she had had a terrible time with her rubbish, and, being a woman of some determination when fired up, she had now firmly resolved to have her say.

The house was brick. The bell was undistinguished. She rang and waited for some time. A woman's voice called out from inside that it was open and you only needed to push. Margaret walked in. The door opened straight onto an open-plan living-room where an astonishingly tall, attractive woman with very long legs stood wearing nothing but a leotard, touching her toes. Loud music, which Margaret recognised to be 'House', played while the doe-eyed beauty stuck her head impossibly deep through her legs. She was unencumbered by fat. She looked the way Margaret had wanted to look before she was married and still worried about such things. She was unselfconscious and stared at Margaret upside-down and through her thighs. Margaret instantaneously disliked her, as she had known that she would, and chose to focus on the woman's less than ample bosom. She was, naturally, bra-less. Her nipples were pert. It made Margaret sick.

'Which do you want to look at?' said the woman, still upside-down, through legs which were straddled and open wide. 'I've got loads.'

Margaret felt, somehow, that the woman was getting the better of her and this caused her to sneeze and embarrass herself. She had always been sensitive to atmosphere.

'I take it that you're after my figures,' continued the woman, but Margaret pulled herself together before she lost sight of her anger entirely. Retrieving her arms from behind her back, she drew them forwards to reveal that she was grasping quite firmly a large, black bin-liner, stuffed full of rubbish. Despite the fact that, even on a cursory glance, she much admired the woman's shag-pile, she strengthened her resolve and tipped the stinking, fetid contents of the bag all over the floor.

'What the fuck did you do that for?' said the woman, drawing herself up with a perfect sense of balance and turning adroitly to face Margaret. 'I thought you'd come to read my meters.'

Margaret had practised her speech for weeks. She was word perfect; she would not allow the woman's bizarre personal conduct to distract her from her moral high ground.

'I am Mrs Smith,' she announced, 'Ms Flower, I presume. And now that I have tracked you down at last, we are going to amuse ourselves by playing a fun little game called "pieces of trash", and you can start the ball rolling by naming that tube.'

'It's a scrunched-up toilet roll holder, I believe,' said Ms Flower, covering herself with a soft, pastel blue towelling robe. 'And I'm quite happy to take your word for it that this is all super fun at your family Christmas dinner, but, madam, I think there must have been some mistake. It is February and I am not your relative. I do not, in fact, know you at all, and I am even less willing to become acquainted with your rubbish.'

'Aha,' said Margaret, surprised at the woman's articulacy. Having heard she was blonde and attractive, she had assumed otherwise. 'But that, unfortunately, has always been the case.'

'Are you going to start chucking used tampons at me?' said Ms Flower. 'Because, if you are, I'm going to just slip into something a little more comfortable.'

'I have built up a rapport with Tina,' Margaret continued in her pre-rehearsed way, she was flustered by both Ms Flower's body and her composure. She wondered if she was undergoing an early menopausal flush. 'And it was she who gave me your address.'

'Tina?' enquired Blondie. 'Who the fuck is Tina?'

'If only you ever appeared at what you undoubtedly call your place of work,' said Margaret, feeling suddenly wrinkled, miserable and old, 'you would perhaps know.'

'Let me offer you a good, strong cup of tea,' said Ms Flower, 'sit down, call me Felicity, for that is my name, and tell me all about it. I'm going out on a hot date later, you know how it is, so I haven't got that long, but you've obviously got something lying heavy in your mind and, of course, if it's nothing but rubbish then I'm your man. But do you think you could possibly take that dustpan and brush and sweep the mess up first, because I'm beginning to find the smell a bit offensive.'

Margaret had the wind taken right out of her sails. She was rather drawn to Felicity's vivacious good nature. It was hard to dislike people who were that physically attractive. You wanted them to appreciate you back. Margaret wished she hadn't missed her Step class for the last three weeks. It was hard when you had children.

She took her regular tea quite strong with only a dash of milk and a plain, digestive biscuit. Felicity didn't have any Hermesetas in the house so it was lucky that Margaret always carried a dispenser unit handy in her purse. The two women sat facing one another, and Margaret exposed her problem area.

After much detective work on the part of Tina, a good friend of Margaret's and the switchboard operator at Wandsworth Borough Council, Mrs Smith had discovered that Felicity Flower was the exclusive Routes' Planning Officer for the dustbin vans of SW11. In Melody Road, the vans always came on the wrong day. Margaret wasn't an unreasonable woman but she had begun to develop a bee in her bonnet about community littering and as her husband had joked, she was clearly allergic to the insect bites. 'Arnold can be very witty,' explained Margaret, who liked to boast about any of her husband's limited achievements.

Felicity asked Margaret what Arnold looked like and Margaret said he was good-looking really. They had been very happily married for eight years now and, before that, they had lived together for five. She had wanted to get married for ages, he'd been resistant to her advances, but she'd caught him now and they'd been very happily married for eight years already.

Felicity pointed out that she'd understood the concept first time round and offered Margaret another digestive.

'You're not married, then?' asked Margaret, realising that Felicity was far too well preserved for the answer to be 'yes', but still trying to uphold some kind of maturity advantage over the sylph. Felicity laughed and replied in the negative. But she said that she was quite prepared to be big-minded about it and accept that maybe she'd just never met the right man.

Margaret said, 'Oh, I know what you mean, men are a pain, aren't they? Arnold really gets on my nerves, sometimes. I know I'd get a lot more done by myself. A lot of my friends who are your age say that what they need is a toy boy and no emotional commitment. You don't throw away your time and energy on useless rubbish when you're not married.'

Felicity laughed and said, 'Touché,' and Margaret realised what she'd said and wanted to kick herself. It was all bloody Arnold's fault. If he wasn't such a drain on her emotional life, she'd never make a fool of herself like that. Men, huh! Tina was better off now her husband had left her, they all agreed. Arnold would never leave Margaret, and that was why she loved him.

Ms Flower, once again, put the kettle on. 'I don't want to rush you,' she said, 'but I've written down your name and address and I've made a note of Wednesdays. Next time I go into the office, I will certainly give it my best endeavours, and I'll make sure to send your love to Tina, so unless you've got anything further to add . . .'

Margaret stared at Felicity.

'I don't want to be personal,' she began, as Ms Flower flinched. 'But, well, I just wondered if there's any special diet you maintain to keep so slim. I know that's really stupid but you look so great and, I would guess, I'm not that much older than you. Gone are the days when I could get to the gym on a regular basis but I thought, well, you know, I just thought you might have a secret you could pass on.'

Felicity was touched.

'That's really a very nice and unexpected thing to say,' she said. 'One person can't possibly ever have any understanding of any other couple's relationship even if they're privy to all the requisite information, and I've certainly never met you before in my life so I don't really feel in a position to give you advice but, well, Margaret, I've always found that the answer is sex. I know that sounds a bit simplistic and, for all I know, you and Arnold do it every day, but I find that a regular regime can cover for a multitude of problem areas. And, of course, I've got a Jacuzzi, although it's a bit of a pain because it's also my regular bathtub and it takes half an hour to fill. Who am I to say? of course, but you did ask me and that's what I feel. Not too much cerebral action and more of the physical. And remember to use a few drops of ylang-ylang. I always find that helps. Perhaps Arnold could buy you some for your birthday after you've played a few rounds of the rubbish game. And now, I'm going to ablute and select my best knickers, so, Mrs Smith, good day to you.'

Margaret went home and waited for Arnold to get in from work. She took him to the new Ikea in Purley. Holding hands while their daughter consumed her Swedish meatballs, they purchased an avocado green step-in bathtub with jet-streamed taps. It always took far too long to fill up and they never bothered to use it.

original sin

Eliza felt she had a Midas touch. Every time she touched a dick it turned to putty. She only had to approach a man and his libido disintegrated before her very best knickers. It was a fucking nightmare not being able to pursue her fucking nightmares. She was at her wits' end and she decided to go to the girls for advice.

First there was Gus, she reminded them, Gus who preferred men. Then there was Giles who could only relate to women on a sexual basis. After that came Jerry Joneth who preferred urination to penetration and then, finally, there was Stan who didn't seem able to relate to women on any kind of sexual level at all.

Felicity said, 'One possible reading of the facts is that all interesting men have sexual problems. That's why I stick to the good-looking dullards. It's my interpretation of safe sex.'

'Come off it, Felicity,' said Madeleine. 'Gus, for one, was very good-looking and, besides, my husband is very interesting and we have great sex on a very regular basis. People say that's what keeps us together, of course, but I think that it's a symptom and not a cause. That's why none of your relationships last more than sixteen hours, Felicity. What Eliza needs is to concentrate her search within a more defined framework. Paul and I will find someone nice for you, Eliza, and I'm going to apply my mind to the problem right this minute. You're not really interested in casual sex, anyway, not like Felicity. Oh no, what you need is a caring, loving, sharing guy and plenty of foreplay.'

'Casual, formal, diagonal, vertical, any kind of sex would suit me fine at the moment. Who can you offer?'

'Madeleine's right,' said Paul. 'I know some guys at work. I'll apply my mind to the problem, too.'

Madeleine said, 'No, sweetheart, I'll deal with this one. You go and pump up the flat tyre on the front driver's side, while Felicity and I give Eliza a few crucial lessons in the creation of sexual tension. Then we'll teach her how to flirt properly and then we'll send her out on a date with someone suitable. Off you go, Paul. You'll find the spare foot pump in the boiler cupboard.'

With Paul judiciously removed from the scene, Felicity and Madeleine began to take the Eliza enterprise seriously. Felicity got the ball rolling by pointing out that the last thing on earth one should do to create sexual tension was to start talking about it. Things had clearly begun to fall apart with Eliza's last admirer, Stan, analysed Felicity, when her friend had agreed to enter into a discussion with him about their potential relationship. 'I'm really surprised I have to remind you about fundamentals like this,' explained Felicity patiently, 'but you either fancy someone, in which case you grab their balls and go for it, or you don't fancy him, in which case there's nothing to talk about it.' There is nothing less sexy, Eliza's kindly friends assured her, than talking about whether or not to have sex.

Eliza pointed out grumpily that it was bloody Stan who had done most of the talking but the girls had no wish to hear the whole dreary saga all over again.

Madeleine sat her friend down with a glass of white wine and began the pro-active part of the training day by showing Eliza how to perch daintily on the edge of a restaurant chair and permit her date to choose the wine. 'Remember that men have fragile egos,' said Madeleine, 'and that they hate to feel exposed or vulnerable where any kind of selection is involved. It makes them feel dominating and masculine to be able to recognise a classic vintage. Do bear in mind that all you have to say is the magic formula, "I don't really mind, only please remember that red wine does tend to give me a headache. I read somewhere that it's to do with the high tannin content," and then let him pick.'

'Man,' cried out Felicity, 'what an absolute pile of unreconstructed, unmitigated drivel. I'm surprised at you, Madeleine. Why the hell would this hypothetical chap be inviting Eliza out in the first place if he didn't want to fuck her at some stage in the evening? What other reason could there possibly be for going out on a date? Take your partner to the local cinema, get him back to your place and then get him in and get your kit off. Simple. Only do remember to get his kit off first so that he can't run away like last time.'

'Don't listen to Felicity,' said Madeleine, pointing out, quite rightly, that Felicity's theory was tragically flawed since Stan had run a mile as soon as they got anywhere near Eliza's bedroom. Eliza became upset at this point and said that there was no need to rub it in.

Madeleine got a new bottle of white wine out of the rack. Grasping its neck firmly between her thumb and forefinger, she demonstrated to Eliza how to rub her hand gently up and down the glass container while pouting her lips in a highly sexual way and simultaneously craning her neck forwards in a goose-like posture. Madeleine said that Eliza was very welcome to take the bottle home and practise the exercise in her own time.

Eliza said that, when she finally got to this mythical restaurant, she thought she might just order a beer, instead. She posed in front of the mirror for a few minutes and the girls gave her points for seductive expressiveness. Eliza began to feel silly.

'Look,' said Felicity, 'we're not trying to preach. We're only trying to say that you're beginning to lose confidence, and then nothing will ever happen. All you have to remember, really, is that there are any number of ways to breach the physical barriers with a man, even if you are a little shy.' She pointed out that no man would ever feel bad if you made a pass at him.

'Neither would I,' pointed out Eliza, 'but nobody ever does.'

Felicity said that Eliza should perhaps turn her hand to a little trick from the beginners' class. 'You take the guy's hand firmly in your own, you turn it over gently so that the palm is facing upwards and then you run your fingers yieldingly along his lifelines as you start to read his fortune. This no doubt involves an imminent and incredibly steamy relationship with a rampantly satisfying but intellectually stimulating young lady. If this goes well, which it surely will, you can then put plan B into action. Grasping the victim's by this stage sweaty hand with a sexuality which will churn away at his heartstrings and arouse his loins no end, you say, charmingly and with a bashful but compelling smile, that, in fact, you know nothing about fortune-telling. The whole exercise was just an excuse to hold his hand. Stan will love it.'

Eliza said it didn't work. He'd withdrawn his hand swiftly and asked for the bill.

As Paul came back into the house, calling out that he'd finished doing the tyres and it wasn't half cold out there, Felicity was in the process of telling Eliza that Stan was clearly an out and out loser and she didn't know why her friend was bothering in the first place.

'What did he do, exactly?' asked Paul eagerly. 'I'm a man.

Maybe I can help.' Madeleine told him not to interfere when the girls were trying to talk. He should go and be helpful and put the kettle on. And perhaps he could pop down to the shops and get some more milk. Paul wasn't stupid. He knew when he wasn't wanted and, claiming to be on the way to the shop, sloped off down to the pub where he bumped into his best mate, Scoop, with whom he had a really refreshing discussion about the lack of technique amongst English centre-forwards of the nineties, and how it was a problem that started at the very lowest level of sporting education where nobody bothered to teach young boys to dribble.

Meanwhile, back at the Academy, Eliza was ready to pass out.

'That's always a good one,' said Madeleine, 'he'll just have to take you in his arms and offer you assistance.'

'I've had enough of this,' said Eliza. 'You're just stultifying me with all this information. I don't know where I'm at. I feel befuddled and paralysed by good advice.'

Felicity said, 'Go with the flow. This is the nineties. You're a modern woman, remember, and there are no rules. It's easy for us to tell you what to do. We've all been there, we all know how difficult it is when it's you and it's actually happening. All I can say is, you're a great girl, get your best knickers on and anyone that doesn't want to have sex with you is, quite frankly, mad. So, if you decide that Stan is what you want, take him. Only don't start talking about it first. His "F" words may be original but they sure aren't going to lead to no sin.'

Eliza sat at home watching the telephone. She hated it when she got into this mood but there didn't seem to be anything she could do to shift the depression. Every time the phone rang she thought it might be Stan. But it wasn't. Every time she popped out for five minutes, she switched on the answering machine, just in case. On her return, when there was no message flashing on the dial, she decided that the machine must be broken. Just like her heart.

Well, that was a bit of an over-statement since she wasn't actually in love, of course. She would feel much worse if that was the case. And she certainly wasn't going to ring him. It was stupid. The ball was in his court now. If he was still keen, he would have to get in touch with her. She watched the telephone for a while longer. She was working herself up into a state. The room was very quiet and her thoughts were very loud. Maybe she should go down and join Paul in the pub, where he was still having a quiet beer with his friend, Scoop, whose brains she had once fucked out in a cemetery. Those were the days. She wondered what had happened to all her incredible self-confidence. She wondered why she was no longer interested in casual sex. She wondered why Stan didn't call.

God, maybe he was sick. Maybe he'd had a bike accident and broken numerous of his most essential bones. Maybe he'd been trying to call all day but there was a fault on the line and he couldn't get through. It could be anything. She decided not to ring the girls to discuss the possibilities in case he was attempting to get through at this very second. She wished she'd paid the extra four quid a quarter for the 'call waiting' facility so that it wouldn't be a problem. She wished that there were some quite rational explanation for his absence when she realised, perfectly well, that there wasn't. Or, at least, not one that she would want to hear. He'd gone to – she couldn't think where he might have gone. She wanted to be reasonable. He had told her how much he cared. He was shy. He had sexual problems. He was gay.

No, she ruled that last one out as melodramatic. She poured herself a gin and tonic and decided that the girls were wrong. She didn't need lessons. The whole thing was a pile of power politics. Stan had never had the slightest intention of getting her into bed. He had caused her to become entangled emotionally through the use of words. And he had merely wanted to know that he could do it. As soon as she had shown the slightest desire to respond, he was satisfied and had dropped her instantaneously, like the dried-out grape which he so closely resembled.

The whole thing stank. She would cut her losses and go down the pub for a drink with the simple-minded but affable Scoop. Which was a good job, too, because she had a jolly good time and there were no messages on the machine when she returned. And she knew it wasn't broken.

planned parenthood

'The thing is,' said Eadie Key, on taking Madeleine and the baby upstairs and showing them both into a room she had prepared especially for such an emergency earlier in the day, 'the thing is that I am eggless.'

Madeleine began to change the stinking nappy and wished, momentarily, that she had been also.

'It's very hard for Albert,' Eadie continued, as Madeleine fiddled with the patently brand-new nappy bucket and its safety-lock plastic lid. 'Albert likes children very much. I know how hard it is for Albert.'

'Oh, but your baby is so beautiful, Maddy,' cooed her husband's long-forgotten relative, as Maddy tried hard to express some fluid. 'I am so glad you could make it here today. I am so sorry that Paul couldn't come and share this reunion with us.'

'Paul was sorry, as well,' lied Maddy as her beautiful baby began to howl uncontrollably and express every possible kind of fluid at the same time.

Eadie had rung her out of the blue. Paul had never been keen to introduce Madeleine to his relatives. She had a vast, extended family of her own and many friends and had, therefore, never been in need of more. She had also always been conscious of the fact that things can never be the same forever. You can't know what might happen tomorrow, let alone in nine months time, she thought looking at the tiny, shrivel of life biting hard at her swollen breast. I might be run over by a bus. Paul might leave me. She had resolved this problem for herself by having two separate lives. Life with her husband was one thing, and it was a very happy thing, indeed. Life with her friends was something quite separate and she had always maintained it that way. She felt this part of herself was self-contained and unbreachable. She knew that Paul would not now leave her, but she had an insurance policy if he did.

And now she was blessed with a third life, where some people only had one. She was incredibly fortunate and totally immersed in her child. Not unhealthily and Paul, of course, adored the child also, but Sophie, she knew, would always be her daughter. She loved her husband, almost with a passion, but this was different. When Sophie was in pain, she wished she were experiencing this pain instead; when Sophie cried, she wished she were crying. She had never felt such an intense sensation of responsibility and protection in her life. She didn't know if she was a good mother, it was too early to tell, and she knew whatever she did would be wrong and that the child would grow up to rebel and resent her, but right now she wanted to be sentimental and even self-congratulatory. She had created a whole new life all by herself and that was a mind-blowing thing to have done. But, it had to be said, she hadn't expected it to be quite such a twenty-four-hour chore. It was rewarding but little fun. She was getting bored.

Eadie was still making absurdly infantile noises and rolling the baby fat around Sophie's knees.

'Oooh, look at her little grip,' said Eadie. 'Look at the way she hangs onto my finger.' Madeleine wondered why everyone she met needed to comment on what was, after all, a reflex action that they themselves had once possessed. It should come as no surprise to them. She arranged her clothing and composed her face. She was not surprised that Paul had always sheltered her from his family. They were, to put it bluntly, most peculiar.

When Madeleine arrived at the house, Eadie was waiting for her eagerly on the doorstep. Since Madeleine was late, she could only assume that Eadie had been standing in the cold for half an hour composing a family portrait with the twins.

The twins were identical. There was Albert, Eadie's spouse, and Frank, his *doppelgänger* of a brother. It was quite remarkable. The three of them stood outside their terraced house in some rather ghastly suburb Madeleine was not familiar with and waved, in unison, as she drew up in the Volvo Estate. They all waved simultaneously with their left hands. They all smiled fixedly with their myopic gazes squinting. They all beckoned her with their gangling hands to come immediately into the house and they rushed over as soon as she had parked, fussing and squawking and offering to help. It was like being in a human hen-house.

'My goodness, my goodness,' squeaked Eadie, 'you are so thin. You are not one of those anorexics, are you? You must be famished. You look positively emancipated.' Frank and Albert rhubarbed their agreement whole-heartedly and ushered Madeleine into the front room, where she saw, before her, the most extravagantly high tea she had ever witnessed. Laid out neatly in great, piled displays there were cucumber sandwiches, thinly sliced. There were egg rolls and cheese dainties and savoury toastlets. She saw plates of home-made scones and Danish pastries and Scotch pancakes. Bowls of extra-thick whipped cream and mixed fruit jams and marmalade and honey and curls of bright yellow butter. Great wedges of chocolate cake sandwiched themselves to cream and butter fillings, topped off with broad shavings of rich, dark cocoa solids. Then there was apple strudel and cheesecake and pecan pie. Lemon meringue, egg custard tart and coffee eclairs. And, in the centre of the whole multi-calorific gastronomic fever there was a massive pink, royally iced, three-tiered cake, its whole top layer covered with Smarties, which spelled out in big, coloured letters the words 'Welcome – Sophi'.

'We are sorry about the "e",' said Albert, or was it Frank? 'we ran out of Smarties.'

'Yes, it's true that we're sorry,' confirmed Frank, or was it Albert? 'we ran out of Smarties.'

'Take her coat, Albert,' blustered Eadie, 'offer to make her comfortable, why don't you?'

'It's Frank,' her brother-in-law corrected her. 'I'm Frank.'

Eadie did not appear to be in the least perturbed by her error. She was blissfully unaware that not to be able to distinguish one's own husband by his appearance alone would be for most women a distressing turn of events.

'How many other people are you expecting?' enquired Maddy, mildly worried about the large number of unknown eccentric relatives to whom she might now be subjected.

But no one else was due to arrive. It would just be the four of them here in the house today. And baby, of course. They all lived together as one happy family and they very much hoped that Madeleine would take a small part of their unity home with them at the end of the afternoon. Madeleine cut herself a slice of something fancy and, her stomach laden with cream, assured them of the obvious. And then Sophie farted and began to cry.

Immediately there was an outcry and a rare hullabaloo.

The men were apoplectic in their desire to be helpful. They ran around picking up chairs and crashing into each other and singing lullabies, curiously not in harmony, and flailing their arms around in a way that could only be described as entirely without coordination. Eadie scolded the boys, who were dressed as if they had not realised that the twentieth century had finally dawned, and, pointing her finger at them in a schoolmistressly way, told them both to behave themselves or she would be forced to give them a jolly good spanking later on. The twins hushed down and began to clear the table and then, while one washed, the other wiped. They continued to whistle in perfect disarray. Eadie, muttering to herself and removing her apron, led Madeleine upstairs and into the bowels of her house while Sophie continued to cry.

The childless woman showed her long-forgotten, fecund relative into the master bedroom, the whole of which was festooned in what Madeleine could only describe as the decor of childhood. The walls were pastel pink and baby blue and the Austrian blinds, as Eadie lowered them 'to protect baby's eyes', stretched down to reveal a full frontal image of Babar and Céleste in a hot-air balloon. They were surrounded by baby elephants. The head of the bed was piled high with fluffy toys and the duvet and pillow covers were white and lacy and embroidered with the slogan 'peaches and cream'. Above the bed hung a framed poster of the cover of a Tintin book, and to its side stood a rocking-chair with a corn dolly tied with silken ribbons to its plain, wooden seat. Most striking of all was the extensive collection of baby accoutrements displayed on the bed. An entire, unopened packet of nappies, a tube of baby wipes, a pot of nappy-rash cream, a bottle-sterilisation kit, and a blanket marked, superfluously, 'nappy-time' were all included in a range superior to Madeleine's own. And, as she walked in and surveyed the scene, Eadie told her repeatedly that she was eggless.

Given the extreme nature of Eadie's enthusiasm for Sophie's welfare, Madeleine would almost have begun to feel worried about the woman's good faith in inviting her for the day, were she not absolutely convinced of the whole family's pathetically inadequate good intentions. There were, as far as she was aware, no other children on this side of the family. The whole of Mothercare had been purchased especially for the benefit of her and her child. Madeleine recognised the generosity of spirit which this implied but thought, unkindly but reasonably, that it was entirely misplaced. She was finding it hard to relax and Sophie, sensing her mother's disquiet, continued to bawl at top volume.

Madeleine realised that the relative had been staring at her offspring in paralysed awe for the last five minutes and felt an intense need to break the silence. She enquired in a disinterested fashion if this was the bedroom of Eadie and Albert, or if they kept it solely as a guest room.

'Oh no,' exclaimed Eadie, bursting into life at the absurd idea that Madeleine had, so amusingly, suggested, 'I don't share a bedroom with Albert.' Naturally, she slept in this part of the house by herself, and as for Albert, she grinned, tickling Sophie under the chin, well, silly old Albert slept in the other bedroom with his twin brother. Of course. Eadie beamed broadly as she stated the obvious and Madeleine, no longer caring that Sophie was still in floods of tears, hurried to finish the job. Accidentally she tipped over the brand-new nappy bucket and the stinking, used wad of cotton tumbled upside down onto the Minnie Mouse rug. Eadie dived head-first to retrieve it.

'It's very hard for Albert,' she repeated, stuck into a speech groove of which Madeleine had heard quite enough already, 'it's very hard for Albert that I am eggless.' Madeleine picked up her possessions, including her child, and covering Sophie's body with her arms to protect her from such an ovarian epsilon fled downstairs to the relative sanity of the unharmoniously chanting, identical twins.

'This is a nut-house,' she commented, as the boys laughed, in unison, at her little joke. She wondered, momentarily, what kind of tricks they played on the complicit Eadie during the midnight hours.

Madeleine rushed for the front door before the scrambled egg had time to descend the stairs. 'We're both very happy that you came,' called out Frank, or was it Albert?

quelling the emotion

I'm a sensitive chap. I know that sounds sort of silly and I realise full well that now you must be thinking, yes, that may well be the case, but we all have our own personal set of insecurity minefields through which to tread our careful paths and what's so special about his? But the thing is that I do have the sense, in some undefined way, that I am particularly prone to stepping on the dynamite.

My job doesn't help, of course. I work in an office in Soho, organising fundraising events for major charities. It's a specialist field. We're market leaders. It's a bit perverse, really, when you come to think about it, that I do a job like that to earn my daily crust, because, actually, I'm a pretty solitary kind of guy. Of course, I like human companionship as much as anyone, I mean, don't we all? But I really don't enjoy any form of group activity. I'm more of a one-on-one sort of person. Groups of people are generally a bit irritating, don't you find? They have a tendency to cater for the LCD conversation. That stands for the lowest common denominator, which makes me sound a bit snotty, and I'm not like that at all, and I hate it when people all gang up and make silly, Carry On jokes with smutty innuendoes. I find it all very juvenile. You two look like an emotionally developed couple, I'm sure you know exactly what I mean.

That's not to say that I haven't got a sense of humour, because I certainly have. Everyone at work tells me what good jokes I make. But I just can't bear it when people without any wit deliver pointless punchlines about nationalities or colours that simply aren't funny, and then the rest of the group joins in and laughs uproariously at some poor, beleaguered section of the community who aren't generally articulate enough to speak up for themselves. It's a self-defence mechanism on the part of these so-called funny people which I, for one, find illuminates only their own inadequacies.

My job doesn't pay well, of course. Nothing worthwhile ever does, but it is important. Well, of course, I know that some people question the moral values behind black-tie events for Third World famine victims and we could just ask people to give donations, but they wouldn't, would they? There's nothing wrong with having a bit of fun, so long as you're serious about it, that's our motto.

No, I'm sorry, I don't think that type of interrogation about my private life is remotely funny. In fact, I think it is very rude indeed. And, quite frankly, it's none of your business, either. I bought the flat as an expression of commitment to a friend of mine, Louise, but now unfortunately I share it with my sister, Eve, because Louise wasn't quite as committed as I was. Don't get me wrong, I wouldn't want to criticise her in any way. She's one of the purest people I've ever met. I would happily have married her; she was wonderful. She was just wonderful. I don't really like talking about myself, I'll have you know, but since you asked, by sheer coincidence I just happen to have a photo of Louise in my wallet. Isn't that odd? She's the one on the left with the spiritual eyes. She does have a certain radiance about her that makes you feel warm inside like chicken soup, don't you think? I hope that doesn't sound in any way pretentious. I'd hate for you to think that I was at all that way inclined – and you must understand that I really hate talking about myself like this, and I wouldn't wish to cheapen what Louise and I shared in any way by exposing it to the public gaze – but, well, and I know this is a bit personal, but when we made love, it was like, like I'd never want to be anywhere else in the whole world for the rest of my life. Like I would just hug her and hug her and feel so much love at the idea of just being near her, just being around her, that I couldn't imagine ever moving away from where she was, ever.

I know you're going to think I'm a bit sentimental now – maybe I am – but it might just be because you've never experienced such a rare and precious thing, you see, because if you had you'd know exactly what I'm trying, rather inadequately I know, to describe. And I wouldn't want that to sound in any way arrogant, because it makes me feel very humble. I know that I'm one of the lucky ones being able to feel these things, which is, of course, why I can't blame Louise for anything of the things that happened next. Not that I want to go into it right now, of course, because, these things are all very complex and there's no simple explanation and obviously this isn't a good moment, but it still has to be said that in an alternative reading of the text she could be said to have humiliated me quite badly. Not in mine, of course. I would never betray her emotional commitment to us both by portraying the profound emotions that we felt for each other in that way, but I can understand why some of my friends considered that she behaved rather badly. Although, as I say, not me. I understand her motives, you see, and, of course, I loved her.

I love her still. I can see now that it was wrong for both of us. I fully agree with her reasoning and I know that she was the brave one and made the right decision for the two of us, although, of course, it was heart-wrenching at the time, but I still feel her inside me, even now and I take comfort from that. I can assure you that she feels the same way, I am convinced of that. Even the pain can be seen in a positive light, when you choose to look at it that way. It's an attitude of mind. Even the hurt can bring you closer, create a new bond, a whole new emotional tie. Yes, I am sorry, thank you very much, that's very kind of you, I'm getting a bit emotional, I do tend to be that way. I know that some English people have a lot of problems with their private repressions and they find it embarrassing when a man gets upset in front of them. But I'm not ashamed to show my feelings; I'm not frightened to tell you that I feel hurt and sorrow. I'm a sensitive person, trying not to step on a mine.

Everyone told me it was a bad time to buy. Well, I suppose it was really. I'm not much of a businessperson and neither is Louise. She simply trusted my judgement and left all the big decisions up to me. I wouldn't normally discuss something as confidential as this with someone like yourself, I'm a very private person, but since you asked and since it's all strictly relevant, the fact is that Louise wasn't working in London at the time and I traipsed around viewing the houses all by myself. The women owners were all very helpful when I explained to them that my girlfriend, who would, of course, be buying the property with me, couldn't be there on that particular day, and so I needed their female point-of-view.

Everyone wants to help the first-time buyers, especially when one's in love.

But, as I say, it was a bad time to buy. I can't blame Louise at all for that aspect of things. She would have done anything not to hurt my feelings and she would simply hate it if she found out that I was losing money over her. She's a terrific girl.

She works for a children's charity, actually, neither of us are very interested in material goods. She loves kids and she'll make a great mother one of these days, when her and Parvin are ready. Parvin's a very nice guy. I only met him the once, of course, and the circumstances were a bit unfortunate, but you can tell that his heart is in the right place. It really cut Louise up badly, I can tell you, having to choose between us like that. It was hard for her, it really was. She wouldn't have done it if it hadn't been the right thing to do, but we both knew that it was. I can tell you, quite frankly, that a lot of tears were shed when we split up, by both parties.

I'm sorry, am I boring you? I don't like talking about myself, as you know, and I'm only too happy to shut up now, and answer any questions you might wish to ask. Yes, I have. I've dropped it by £20,000 actually. And Louise's mother, who liked me enormously, made these curtains for us both and I've included them in the price, also. They're really well made, Louise's whole family is immensely talented. Very creative people and I got on well with all of them.

Yes, I'm afraid so, electric. Louise is more of a cook than I am. If she'd stayed, I would have made the effort and gone over to gas, but, well, I lost heart without her. But I met a girl recently, and I'm feeling quite hopeful. She's called Eliza. I'm taking it slowly this time, of course, because although I'm completely over Louise in every way, and I never think about her, ever, well, I just wouldn't want to jump into anything too quickly. I care about Eliza enormously, of course, and she's a terrifically talented girl. And very interesting too. Very cultured. She lectures in anthropology at London University and she's written quite a well-received paper on the tribal rituals of menstruation. I really respect her for what she does. Louise's work is very stimulating, too, of course. Not that I'm comparing the two of them. I wouldn't dream of doing anything quite that crass. It would be invidious and very unfair on both of them. They're totally different people and incomparable in every way. Louise was very sensitive, of course, and more like me, but

Eliza is also sensitive, naturally, only in a very different way.

I get the feeling that Eliza is very experienced sexually. Not that it makes any difference to me. Louise had only had one long-term boyfriend before she started going out with me so that was all a very different kettle of fish. But it's good to be experienced. You know what you want. You don't need to be guided. And I think that's great. Eliza is a very self-contained person, of course, and I do find her tremendously attractive. But I do think that we should take things slowly at first. I wouldn't want her to rush into anything when she isn't ready. It's very important to me that she should know what she wants, that she should feel I'm not pressurising her into anything when she's not entirely happy about it.

Yes, that's right, that one's my sister's room. She lives in there with her boyfriend now and that's part of the reason that I'm selling the house. I couldn't afford the mortgage by myself and I asked her to come and live with me but she arrived lock, stock and barrel with boxes of stuff and boyfriend in tow. He's a nice enough guy but he's no good for her and there's no point trying to discuss it, she won't listen. It's not that I'm fussy but he doesn't go to work; he never seems to actually do anything and he never lifts a finger around the house. What I think is that there are ways to wash and there are ways to dry but Jake doesn't seem to be familiar with either. Louise was really good at the washing-up, of course, but she's hardly going to return home for the sake of the crockery. You see, I have got a sense of humour. I can make good jokes when I want to.

The whole situation is very sad, though, because I used to be so close to my sister before she started going out with this layabout. I'm not at all judgemental but it can't be much of a relationship, can it? They're locked into the bedroom day after day, never coming out except to have a bath together, which I think is disgusting, but they laugh and splash about and tell me not to complain because it saves on the water, and once they're behind closed doors they shout and yell and they're obviously fighting like cat and dog and it's very destructive for both of them. You can hear them at it all night, abusing the furniture Louise's mother gave us, going at each other with real venom. It's just awful to hear. And she always used to be so proud and anti-violence. It's really ironic that it's all come to this, in what would have been Louise's room, of course, had things turned out differently. But, well, obviously they didn't.

I do realise that what I just said was a bit stupid but I'm feeling a bit frazzled. Jake and Eve were making particularly heavy weather of their relationship last night, and I'm the one who always seems to be left feeling the worse for wear. They've grown so used to it that they're immune. They just get up in the morning, smiling away like nothing's been going on all night, and then they make each other breakfast in bed as some sort of reconciliation. It's just got to be so bad for both of them.

Louise didn't see it like that. She was more tolerant than me. She used to talk to Eve a lot in private and try and sort things out with her. Our whole relationship, in fact, came to a head after yet another of Eve and Jake's spectacular nocturnal fights, which is partially why I feel some quite justifiable resentment towards the couple. I lay there in bed that night, trying to get some shut-eye and Louise was by my side, twisting and turning and moaning quite loudly. I told her that we both just had to ignore the noise and that she should use the Sleep-Tite ear plugs I had bought for both of us. Louise hugged me close and, telling me that she had cramp, suggested that I put her ear plugs into her drums for her. It was all a bit tricky in the dark. She held me very close and said that once again she was finding it quite impossible to go to sleep. We'd both been sleeping in this room for quite some time now, she said, and things were not improving in any way. She snuggled up to me, resting her wonderful, chestnut hair over the arc of my chest. I told her that I knew how hard it was but she should just rise above it and get some well-earned sleep. If she gave up the job in Bolton, I pointed out, then she could come and live with me permanently and we could get rid of Eve and her loathsome snake.

Louise murmured an inaudible reply as she began to settle down and doze off, but then the unbelievable caterwauling started up all over again. Bang, bang, crash, yodel. It was quite unbearable. Louise simply couldn't take any more. She sprang up and out of the bed in a frenzy and she cried out that it was no good, she couldn't take any more, it was driving her crazy, something had to be done. Despite my efforts to calm her and the soothing way I stroked her shoulders to release some of the tension, she was really feeling the pressure. She had reached the end of the line physically, she said, and she was going to sleep downstairs on the sofa where she wouldn't feel quite such an overwhelming sense of frustration. I quite understood, I told her, but it obviously made more sense for me to stay upstairs and get some kip, since there was only enough room on the sofa for one person to have a good night's sleep and the noise didn't bother me quite as much as it did her. She was clearly too furious to speak and she went storming downstairs without being able to utter a word.

When I joined her in the kitchen in the morning, she was already packing up her things to leave. She had had a long chat with Eve, she said, and all of a sudden it had dawned on her that she didn't have to put up with this. She wasn't a victim. She had choices and she had just made one. She was very close to me, she said, and she didn't doubt for a second that I loved her. No, there's no need to doubt that, I assured her, not for a second. But we had to face up to the fact that our relationship had to overcome a whole, massive problem area and I was clearly not going to be the one to resolve it. She simply couldn't take it any more. She was leaving.

So that's why I'm selling. I know Louise is going out with Parvin now. I fully accept that and I'm not seriously thinking that it won't continue to be the case. And I'm sort of dating Eliza, too, of course, and that's important to me because I really respect her and so I have to take her feelings into account. If I manage to sell the house, I can buy a little flat with a smaller mortgage and I'll be able to get rid of Eve. Which is not to say in the least that I'm selling so that Louise will come back, which would clearly be a ludicrous thing to think and on the outer realms of realistic possibility. I know that she has gone. It would be stupid to think otherwise. But Eve and her dreadful boyfriend were the problem area and whatever happens with whoever in the future, I wouldn't want that woman to be subjected to the same torments as Louise. It's just not fair. She has suffered enough and I have found out something about myself and gained something from the experience. Quite frankly, it's a lot of unhappiness for nothing if you don't choose to see it that way. And, not that I'll ever get back together with Louise, of course I won't, but, just supposing, hypothetically, for a moment that I did, or that I was going out with anyone else for that matter, then I can't afford to run the risk of losing this rare and precious gift of natural communication all over again. It's just too upsetting. So, to cut a long story very short, that's the reason that I'm selling at such a cut-price bargain figure. Now tell me honestly, you've had a good look round, are you at all interested? Look, don't rush into anything, I know how hard it is, there's no need to come to a decision right away. Go home, take some time to think about it. But I can assure you that you won't find more space for your money anywhere in this part of town. If I wasn't desperate, I wouldn't sell and I'm really sincere about that. This would make an ideal home for someone who's interested in bedrooms.

Look, I'm sorry, I'd love to chat some more but I'll have to rush you, I'm supposed to be going out to dinner this evening to meet some of Eliza's friends. That's my new girlfriend, you understand, we're just working our way into the relationship gradually. Taking things one step at a time. I really don't want to hurry you, and it's been a pleasure to meet you and show you around and answer all of your questions. And I do so much hope that you like it. For the right couple this would make an ideal home. I am sorry, I didn't mean to get upset. I do get that way sometimes, I'm a very sensitive guy.

reverse half-angel

Kurt said, 'Do it for ten, ladies, show me some pain,' and Felicity, who had always been flexible, promptly fell in love. The acoustics in the Space were poor so Kurt had to shout out loudly above the sound of an African bongo band rehearsing in the studio next door, and, as he uttered the instructions in his softest, sexiest West Country accent, all the heterosexual girls swooned and thought he was Apollo incarnate. He resembled a trendy, bohemian version of a Chippendale with his dark grey, skin-tight one-piece and his funny green and red felt joker's slippers with their soft jangling bells hanging from the toes and tinkling gently as he cut a swathe around the room. He was slightly balding, in a premature kind of way, but this did nothing to detract from his charms, which were many and all highly visible. Felicity inhaled the athletically charged atmosphere and congratulated herself heartily on the wise decision to add static trapeze to her already varied collection of performance skills.

'This preliminary strengthening exercise will help you a lot,' said Kurt, 'since you'll never get anywhere without that extra bit of push.' Felicity, generally speaking, found vulgar men unattractive and so, with a withering glare at Kurt, turned her attention to the practice sheet he had handed her on arrival and she continued to pursue her eternal quest for self-fulfilment.

'You two new girls aren't really size-compatible,' said Kurt, introducing Felicity to a slip of a girl whose name was Emily, 'but it won't matter much if it's just for the strengthening.' Emily was spry and petite and properly kitted out. She immediately explained to Felicity that she was actually a jazz singer. Felicity said that it must be great to have such a fulfilling profession and she added that she liked jazz a lot although it was one of those genres that you had to know an awful lot about before you could work out where it was coming from. Emily was sympathetic.

'We should talk about this some time,' she said. 'Every medium becomes easy when you know how to listen.'

Kurt called out that he wanted to see a little less listening and a bit more strengthening going on over there in the corner because this was a serious activity for serious people.

'Oh ho,' laughed Felicity, 'don't be so pompous, Mr Teacher. It's perfectly possible to be quite serious and yet have some fun at the same time, don't you think?'

Emily laughed and the two girls immediately bonded in their united derision for the underhung instructor. 'Just a little bit camp,' they agreed, and worried about his sexuality. 'He's feeling threatened and needs to vocalise his fears.'

'But you never know, Felicity,' Emily said in her perky,

ingenuous way, 'this might just be your lucky night. You're a very attractive girl, I expect you get the pick of the crop.'

The other girl laughed and told Emily not to be stupid. Emily was far prettier than she was. Felicity's feet were flat and her bum was enormous, while Emily, on the other hand, was perfectly proportioned. She had an hour-glass figure. Both the girls were loving it; nothing could hinder their budding friendship now.

Kurt came over and taught them an exercise that he referred to as 'stripping the cat'. Using her knees as a hinge, Felicity hung from the wooden bar upside down, straightened her legs, brought them off the bar into a pike position and then right over her head. Emily, who had the difficult task, heaved loudly and tried to push Felicity's whole body through her arms and back up to the bar. Felicity, ill-prepared for such a corporeally challenging manoeuvre, felt the blood rushing to her face and, as she hung by her hands for dear life, her loose and flapping T-shirt fell hopelessly over her head to reveal a pair of perfectly formed but entirely naked breasts. Both girls thought this was absolutely hilarious and as Kurt shifted uneasily and told the girls to pull themselves together, Emily and Felicity began to laugh uproariously and, together, held the T-shirt high and helped Felicity to ease herself off the trapeze.

'God, that was exciting,' said Felicity, her face bright red. But the teacher didn't hear since he had already turned away from the newly formed partnership to deal with a much older one.

'Kurt,' called out the girls, feeling that some personal tuition was what they required.

'I have been called worse,' he replied, jogging back towards them, his little balls jangling for all they were worth. They asked him what to do next and he stressed the importance of doing ten of everything. 'And when you get to the end of the first ten, you do another ten, only this time much faster. That's the way to build up power,' he explained, 'the key is over-exertion.'

'I always like to over-exert,' said Felicity, and the two girls once again started giggling symbiotically. Kurt was beginning to find the pair irritating and he told them that they should both go and ask Helena, an advanced pupil, how to climb a rope while he helped silent Jim and sullen Judy to practise some drops.

As Felicity and Emily turned back to the trapeze, Helena, on hearing her name, climbed down from her rope and leaped across onto Kurt's elastic waist, clinging to his side like a chimpanzee. She gazed at her mentor adoringly and the two of them began to make smoochy noises whilst she flipped her head and torso suddenly backwards and hung upside down from his waist, grasping with her thighs alone. It was nauseating. Helena lowered both of her hands onto the floor, took her body weight into her shoulders and then quite unexpectedly flipped her legs away from Kurt's body, leaving herself in an unsupported but perfectly poised handstand. She walked away from the three of them on her flattened palms and Kurt applauded her athleticism roundly.

'You two are absolute beginners,' he said to Emily and Felicity, who had never claimed otherwise. 'You won't be able to do anything like that for months.' And then he followed Helena over to the trampoline where they promptly lost interest in the rest of the class and bounced around for a few minutes, Kurt's balls jangling wildly all the while.

Emily said she hated girls who behaved like that. It was pandering to all the worst foibles of the male species. Felicity said she didn't think it had much to do with gender. Helena was obviously an exhibitionist and a bloody show-off. And, not that she knew much about it, of course, but Helena's rope-climbing technique had left much to be desired.

The two girls carried on with their exercises, chatting amiably. If you take up a regular activity, they agreed, you should either have a friend in the class, or decide that you fancy the teacher. It gave you that extra stimulus that you needed to attend each week. Certainly wasn't going to be the latter, they both joked simultaneously, and then they laughed some more and felt glad that they had each found themselves a new kindred spirit at the most unlikely of venues. Emily explained about being a jazz singer. 'When you've found your medium, you should stick with it,' she said. She knew that she had found hers.

Felicity had never had the chance to perform in public, she told her friend, although she had often had a roll around in the grass as a young woman, and she had frequently engaged in activities that involved the implicit trust of a partner. When she had popped in to the circus school to check out the classes the previous week, she had explained her position to the curly-headed man in administration. He had told her that static trapeze would suit her down to the ground. He hoped that she didn't think he meant that she would fall off, he added in sudden confusion, because he hadn't meant that at all. He just hoped, well, he was tying himself in knots now, and he was finding it hard to finish his sentence but, anyway, he was sure she knew what he meant. Felicity replied that tying oneself in knots had always been, in her experience, a highly pleasurable one. As she wrote out a cheque for the first three classes, the terrified man in administration made a mental note of her name.

Emily said she hadn't encountered Goldilocks herself. A particularly admiring fan, who had approached her after her last gig and asked her to autograph his funny bone, had told Emily about the school and she had been immediately interested in extending her repertoire. Felicity laughed some more and said she didn't need to state the obvious. The two women next took it in turns to lie on their backs on the trapeze, support each other by the ankles and then let go, leaving the performer balanced solely on the ridge of the buttocks. It looked spectacular but was merely a question of faith and concentration. Once in position, Felicity smiled to herself in delight but the joking had stopped.

Kurt and Helena returned to the fold.

'That's excellent,' said Kurt. 'And now we're going to learn some shapes.'

'I know circles,' said Emily

'And I know squares,' said Felicity.

Kurt wondered if it was possible to expel pupils for getting on too well on their first lesson. Instead he chose a more divisive option and decided to teach them the Bird's Nest. Felicity went first. Having tucked her T-shirt well in to her leggings, she hung upside down from the ropes above the bar and arched her back. Kurt told her to remove one leg and the opposite arm from the ropes and to twist her hips around so that her body was balanced in a straight line underneath the bar. Cautiously Felicity did so and then, holding her leg, Kurt guided it over her body and under the bar, so that she then formed exactly the same, supposedly graceful, shape, but now facing in exactly the opposite direction.

'I can't do it,' said Felicity, 'I'm going to fall.' Kurt told her not to be silly. It was mind over matter and you couldn't ever know if you were capable until you gave it a go. She was looking good, he said, and she had to believe in her own potential. Felicity strove to hang on but her body wasn't twisted far enough around, her legs got stuck, her hands gave way and she let go of the trapeze, collapsing helplessly underneath it into Kurt's protective embrace.

'I told you I couldn't do it,' she said, grumpily, but, lying cradled in Kurt's solid, comforting limbs, she wasn't entirely sure that the shape had failed. Kurt pulled himself together abruptly and placed Felicity firmly back on her own two feet. Reverse half-angel had been a mutually satisfactory experience.

Emily broke the silence, bringing the whole touching cameo to a close. Felicity shouldn't hog the whole lesson, she pointed out, but kindly. It was her turn now, she said, but she, for one, felt that she could manage on her own. From time to time, said Kurt, that was the best way to be. He'd never quite managed to work out for himself which was better. It was so much a question of mood and intuition and that was something you could never predict. But it was getting close to eight o'clock, now, he added, and it was very important that they shouldn't forget to do the wind down. He was very glad that the two of them had joined the class. He hoped they understood why he discouraged too much frivolity. If you didn't take trapeze seriously you would get hurt, but if you did it was the most satisfying thing you could do with two ropes and a wooden bar. The two of them were made for each other. From the context, it wasn't absolutely clear which two Kurt meant, but Emily and Felicity were already a team and they didn't need to ask.

sympathetic stuffing

Claude looked up from the deck of the speedboat and out towards the deep, blue sea of the Gulf of Mexico and realised that he must have made the right choices in life. He lounged around, resplendent in his blue and white striped captain's outfit and gazed lovingly at the natural world surrounding him.

In the old days, in the city, with the smog and the gridlock and the constant clamping of his BMW, Tuesday would have meant a heavy meeting with Bruno or a serious session with Algernon. But now, luxuriating in his private, aquamarine haven,

Tuesdays – just like Mondays or Thursday or Sundays – meant caring for sea-cows. He picked up his binoculars, scoured the horizons for signs of life and considered, contentedly, that he must, surely, have stumbled upon heaven.

Ever since the day on which Claude's mother had given him a green stuffed version of the creature as a wee infant in the Highlands, Claude had loved the manatee. Aged seven, he could not possibly have understood the problems concomitant with being one of the world's most endangered animal species, but, lying in his bed, he did understand what a source of comfort the creature could be. He hugged his soft, furry friend while the north wind blew and the Gulf Stream shadows flickered frightfully on his bedroom wall. And then, quite unexpectedly, Claude's father acquired gainful employment and the whole family moved lock, stock and barrel to a council flat on the outskirts of Leith. In the ensuing chaos, the child lost his favourite toy.

Eventually, as do all God's creatures, Claude grew up. In the process he realised that he, too, would be considered to be a member of a minority species. Having always thought of himself as an insignificant cog in the main body of humanity, this marginalisation came as something of a shock to the system. Claude, whose name at that time was something quite different and considerably more brutish-sounding, was bewildered by the discovery that people to whom he had never spoken in biology or who had never picked him for their team in netball could suddenly regard his insubstantial presence in the school playground as an object of derision. Girls whom he had never once snogged at a school disco would giggle at his handwriting and offer to lend him their lipstick. Some of which was rather nice. Claude was forcibly reminded of his absent companion. Perhaps, when he got older, he too could lose himself in the move away from home.

Years later, now relabelled Claude and sporting a head of dyed-blond hair and a silk blouson jacket, the former victim of minor players in the field of power often explained to his many friends in the Florida Keys that he had woken up one day knowing that his existence as a dealer in small leather goods was utterly without meaning. He hadn't suddenly realised that there was more to life than crocodile wallets, he had known all along that there had to be. But he had never had the internal strength to follow that belief. And once he had come to terms with it, the decision had been easy.

Claude had followed not his dreams but his sympathies, which had, eventually, led him to the scarred and stinking corpses of sea-cows in the south-eastern United States. Motorboats hurtled over their slow-moving bodies and made permanent tracks on their flesh. Man has been here, they said, man has made his mark.

Claude cried easily. In his manatee reserve, surrounded by the crippled victims of speed, he cried often. His new career didn't make him feel good, he wasn't that arrogant. It just made him feel less bad.

Claude descended into his cabin and got dressed. A little flamboyant gear was called for. He was going to meet a local senator who would, perhaps, donate large sums of money to Claude's reservation if he felt that there were votes involved. So Claude, who had learned a lot about PR in his years as sexual service industry to some of its leading executives, knew that the photo opportunity was all-important.

On a bank filled with stinking reeds at the edge of a swampy marsh, a tall fellow with a southern accent and a silly hat boomed out his support for the world's oppressed peoples. There was a parallel that could be drawn, pronounced the senator, between the starving masses of the oppressive Marxist regime of Cuba and the blighted and vulnerable creatures of the fetid swamp. Claude didn't care what parallels were drawn as long as the senator coughed up some money, and so, smiling politely, he closed his eyes and blocked his ears and tried hard not to think of England.

After the speeches, the senator took Claude over to the hospitality tent for a glass of punch and some strawberries. The afternoon was a benefit. Rather curiously, then, and just as the senator was telling Claude about his projected plans for a chain of nature reserves all the way up the Keys, each for a separate, very worthy, but highly sympathetic cause, a photographer wandered over to where the two of them stood. He was stocky and dark and had a Welsh accent.

'I recognise you,' he said. 'You're the guy from the scandal, aren't you?'

Claude made no attempt to hide the fact. He had made a lot of money from the sexual pleasuring of others and all parties had gained from the experience. The senator shifted about on his patent leather toes. They were new, these shoes, and they hurt. His wife had bought them and forced him to wear them. They were giving him corns and he was finding it hard to concentrate. He hoped very much that his smile looked sincere in the publicity shots. His wife, Desirée, had warned him about getting involved in a cause whose leader had a suspect sexuality and an even more suspect past. It wasn't Christian, she had sniffed. It may win a few votes with those people, but make sure not to go anywhere near his wineglass.

The senator knew that his wife was a delicate creature. As a child, in Phoenix, Arizona, she had suffered from lupus and had never been able to go out in the sun. She was the kind of wafer-transparent woman who made his heart weak and his skin flushed. She needed looking after. She wasn't good but she sure was feeble. For her birthdays he gave her chocolates and soft, pastel-coloured flowers without ugly, garish blooms.

'It was me and my wife's wedding anniversary, yesterday,' he said suddenly to a surprised Claude and the hairy photographer, who was now stuffing his face with free barbecue food.

'Really?' asked Claude, to whom these rituals were meaningless.

'Really?' asked the photographer, for whom these rituals were meaningless, because he had no one with whom to share them.

'We've been married for eleven years,' said the senator.

'Congratulations,' said Claude casually while the photographer poured on more relish. 'Did you do something nice to celebrate?'

The senator had had a busy day. He hadn't been able to get out to the shops. He'd wanted to take Desirée to the new Mexican place on the waterfront for a special romantic supper by candlelight, but it had been hard to fit it all in to his schedule. He had so many meetings, now, and so many commitments. Life was hard. And he received a parking ticket outside the office. By the time he left it was far too late to think about food. Desirée was delicate and fussy about what she ate. Which was, generally, nothing at all after ten PM. Dinner lay heavy on her stomach and she would moan softly all night and ask her husband to fetch her a hot-water bottle, which was an item she had discovered on a shopping trip to Britain and whose use she had forced her husband to pursue with vigour ever since.

He stopped for gas on the way home. He loved his wife, he loved his job, he loved his country, he loved his car. He wondered why it was so hard to deal with all four at the same time. Were he to include Nancy, that would make five, but today she didn't count. It was his anniversary, after all. Shit. It was his anniversary. Nine forty-five at night, eleven years of marital bliss and he was on his way home without a gift. Fuck. Desirée was sure to be up all night with the hot-water bottles. Even worse, so would he. The senator looked around the gas station. There had to be something, some small item which could lay claim to signify love or at least affection. His eyes lit on a shelf, somewhere inside the service booth, high above the head of the greasy man behind the till. Through the top-security glass, in the eye of the infra-red security camera, the senator pointed at the only purchasable object on display. It was covered with dust. It was a cuddly toy.

The man behind the till recognised the senator, whose policies he did not like. He hoped that the swipe machine would reject the politician's credit facilities and embarrass him in public. But it did not. The senator used the cuff of his lambswool sleeve to brush away the dust from his acquisition and then he drove away into the night.

'We didn't do anything,' said the senator. 'I'm sure you know what it's like, being a busy man yourself.'

'Oooh, I do, I do,' said Claude.

'But,' said the senator, 'it was all okay in the end because I bought her a fabulous present, which she really loved. Funnily enough, it was rather appropriate to today's engagement. It was a stuffed manatee.'

Claude smiled. He had been through his stuffed manatee phase. Now he preferred the live ones.

taking it on the rise

Madeleine has always considered herself to be a powerhouse in the fast lane. Regularly she ploughs up and down the pool at her local gym, counting out her designated twenty-two lengths in loud, regular rhythms (though on occasions she gets bored and cheats and prematurely rewards herself with a steam bath in the menthol-filled cubicle next door). She still has a perfectly acceptable figure for a woman of her age and, as she lies on the white plastic bench in her crinkly, peach-coloured one-piece, fellow sweaters admire her mature curves to their full advantage.

Splayed out unselfconsciously in the eucalyptus fog, Madeleine observed her body carefully for signs of ageing and, not wishing to dwell too long on unsightly fat, she turned her attention to the appearance of unsightly hair. Felicity had repeatedly told Madeleine that hair was a feminist issue. Quite regularly she made no attempt to clear away her hirsute hollows. Madeleine was not persuaded by this argument. Felicity should appreciate that cleanliness is next to godliness and that smooth, silken skin, in any event, goes some way towards the effective attainment of physical perfection. Staring down at the condensation dripping from her inner thigh, Madeleine became acutely aware that the time for perfection was ripe.

Dana, the beauty consultant, is South African and was wearing a white overall with large pockets into which she placed metal instruments with great care, taking pains not to chip any one of her immaculately attended fingernails.

'And how are you?' she asked Madeleine, recognising her face from what they both euphemistically call their many previous consultancies. Madeleine, as always, replied that she was fine and climbed onto the treatment bench with one leg bent and one leg flat, bracing herself for the onset of tearing pain.

'My, my,' said Dana, 'those are some impressive tufts you have there. Strong and resilient, just like Madeleine herself,' she added, 'and you can tell a lot about people's state of mind from their roots.'

'Oh,' laughed Madeleine, feeling flattered, and she told Dana, not for the first time, that never once in her whole life had she considered the removal of hair from her lower legs (although she always made a point of shaving her armpits before swimming).

Madeleine enjoys this section of the ritual. She thinks of it as the warm-up period before the storm and watches Dana who is now bustling around the room in her hygienist's gear, preparing spatulas and laying out tissues. Madeleine is totally overcome by the process and is overwhelmed by the sensation that in Dana's capable hands everything will turn out for the best in the best of all possible worlds.

Outside Dana's office a sign advertises the fact that Dana is involved in the business of 'beauty therapy'. Dana considers that her chosen career is not just about the body and that an integral part of her job is to listen and to reply in confidence but never to contradict. Dana began today's encounter by asking her client whether she had been busy lately. She was in some doubt as to Madeleine's occupation but this was immaterial. She recognised Madeleine's tufts and fishes, vaguely, as clues from one of her regulars. She knows that Madeleine knows that she does not know. It is a tacit part of the unspoken professional contract between them.

Madeleine smiled and said, 'Well, in my line of work we're not so affected by the recession.' Dana turned away and retrieved from her trolley a wooden spatula more readily associated with choc 'n' nut in the back row. Unless you're Madeleine's husband, Paul, of course, in which case you buy the jumbo popcorn, which you insist on finishing to the very last kernel and which makes you both nauseous. 'And what do you do?' asked Dana, entering, at last, into the spirit of the game.

'Oh,' said Madeleine, considering her options. In December she was a general practitioner with a bent towards the homoeopathic side of things. She was having a lot of trouble with some of her more sceptical patients, particularly men, who had been dissatisfied with her prescription of lavender baths and pulsatilla. Last autumn, with the onset of October doldrums, Madeleine had been a choreographer of modern dance and utterly fed up with the rigid, gender-defined structures of contemporary ballet, heartily desirous of creating her own brand-new powerful and anti-romantic forms. She had become quite heated in her doom-laden forecast for modern movement and Dana had listened with a keen interest and explained to Madeleine that, as a child in the Transvaal, she had taken tap lessons for years. But now she was saving up every penny to buy a flat in Maida Vale.

Earlier still, Madeleine had been a teacher, simple and dedicated but weighed down by the burdens of under-disciplined teenagers, absent parents and multiple extra-curricular activities. Dana had sighed sympathetically and said that she knew exactly how Madeleine felt. Her mother was a teacher in Cape Town and, growing up in the Transvaal, she had determined to make something more of her life, adding her own insignificant contribution to the total sum of world beauty.

'Don't you miss the weather?' Madeleine had asked as Dana became suddenly and quite unusually animated, violently tearing great chunks from her normally soothing wad of cotton wool.

'Yes,' said Dana, 'but I do try and get home as often as possible to visit my folks and feel the space around me. Clark doesn't ever come,' added Dana. 'He has objections. Which is silly really.'

Madeleine listened out over the months and years but Dana never again mentioned the truculent Clark. Now Dana talked instead about her eternal search through the streets of Maida Vale, with prices constantly tumbling and an ever-increasing number of rooms appearing in the same price range. 'You shouldn't peak too late,' Madeleine told Dana helpfully. 'It's a great time to enter the market, but if you want a bargain it's imperative that you take it on the rise.'

'Just like your tufts,' said Dana. And Madeleine, realising that the delicate operation was about to commence, tucked the single piece of tissue immodestly into her bikini line in order that the hot wax that Dana would imminently apply should not scald her more erogenous zones.

Dana placed the chamois cloth strip onto Madeleine's only too visible bikini line hair and the patient prepared herself for therapy. In one fell and swooping motion, Dana pulled the strip of material up and away and then, staring at the bristle-clotted cloth with an expression of tender satisfaction, patted her client's reddened skin with moisturising cream.

'All finished,' she said as Madeleine gratefully looked down at her smooth and balded inner thigh. 'You can put your clothes back on now.' Dana was smiling but Madeleine felt cheated. The therapist had worked too fast and the patient hadn't yet had the chance to become a creatively fulfilled woman.

unsustainable positions

Quite unexpectedly, Eliza suddenly found herself in a position she could not happily sustain. With her behaviour irrational, her moods swinging wildly and her body flushing hot and cold in tidal waves of irregular emotion, she spent large periods of each long and empty day staring at her telephone or simply blankly into mid-air. She had told herself with an iron resolution that never again in her whole life would she set her bulbous, bloodshot eyes on Stan's crustaceous face and yet, inexplicably, here she was approaching dinner in fourth gear and clinging to his side in a desperate attempt to read affection into his every malco-ordinated move. It was a disaster and there was only one conclusion. How could it have happened? She had taken so much care to cover every wrinkle in her body with emotional Durex and yet, still, she suffered the slings and arrows of her tragic flaw; she was in love.

Paul opened the door in his utterly professional manner and Eliza gestured vaguely towards Stan, introducing him as her friend. She had pre-warned the girls not to evidence surprise at the appearance of the man to whom she had unwittingly entrusted her heart. He wasn't her usual type, she had said. He more closely resembled the kind of roughage one would normally eat with yoghurt for one's breakfast. Immediately aware that this must be Muesli Man, Madeleine, the hostess with the mostest, graciously beckoned the couple into a room which Stan immediately noticed to be chock-a-block with modern, graphite-framed art. Despite Madeleine's best endeavours to wean Eliza off an admirer whom, on aural evidence alone, she had concluded must be wiltingly impotent, she did want to play an active role in Eliza's romance. Stan did not look like a romantic hero. He clucked and fussed about his designated place in the evening's proceedings.

'Oh, anywhere you like,' said Paul, who had always been remarkably insensitive to the prevailing social wind. 'And how was your date with my mate, Scoop?' Paul asked Eliza, displaying his habitually misplaced enthusiasm. He had been dying to find out but could hardly ask his friend. Eliza's skin, almost imperceptibly, grew pinker and Paul demanded to know the reason for her uncharacteristically coy behaviour. Eliza gazed solemnly at the parquet flooring and wondered why she ever chose to ask for advice from a friend who had elected to marry such a blundering fool.

But Madeleine and Paul were happy. Ever since the unforgettable day on which the advertising whizz-kid had reprioritised his life and asked the gorgeous and elegant Madeleine to become his charming bride, he had been overcome by the romantic sensibility that every one of his friends, whatever their personality and whatever they might think that they thought, would be so very, very much happier if they could only experience the same kind of personal, domestic bliss as he. On his wedding day, he had been thrilled to manoeuvre a situation in which Scoop would serve as best man and Eliza as bridesmaid. Affectionately, that life-changing morning, he had crossed Madeleine's fingers and told her to hope for the best. Scoop needed the love of a good woman, he said, and although he himself couldn't and now, of course, would never know quite how good Eliza was, any friend of his wife's was good enough for Scoop.

Just a few special moments after Paul and Madeleine started the evening's swinging to the sound of a tune they would continue to request in piano bars at all the world's most romantic beach resorts for the rest of their lives, Scoop and Eliza led the rest of the dancers to the fully-sprung floor. Paul considered that they made a lovely couple and insisted that the scene be reshot three times. The video was perfect but, alas, the love story was not to be. After the ceremony the pair never saw one another again although the groom, in his heart of hearts, still cherished secret dreams of foursomes in a house-share in the hills behind Malaga. After many years spent in the careful perusal of mortgage options on the inside-back pages of available timeshare colour supplements, he had, once again, tried his hand at channelling the vagaries of love.

With a squeak across newly varnished pine, Eliza's guest shifted his pear-shaped buttocks and Paul could not establish where Eliza had found this particular member of her constantly shifting love entourage. Stan, observed Paul, was neither musclebound nor inarticulate enough to be one of Eliza's lovers but he still felt sorry for tonight's victim and hoped that the girls would not start exploring his male vulnerabilities and indulging in the kind of raucous degeneracy that Paul considered to be impenetrably feminine. 'Stan,' he said, fearing that the worst was yet to come, 'sit next to me over here, you'll be safe at this end of the table.' And, as Stan serpentined for cover by Paul's gel-slicked side, the final guest cannonballed herself into the room.

Stan kissed and touched the startlingly attractive Felicity and made a valiant attempt to look as if physical contact came to him quite naturally. He cared about Eliza very much and sensed that friendship was important to her. On some levels, he was a perceptive man.

Felicity was starving and clamoured for food. She was on a high, she told her boisterously appreciative friends, as she had been practising her erotic trapeze cabaret act with Emily, her new partner, for hours. She was keen to demonstrate her accomplishments in public at every available opportunity, she said, winking violently at an astonished Stan, but to perform with any sense of satisfaction, she added, 'I do so need a man.'

Madeleine began to feel sorry for the terrified member of the evening's entertainment.

'And do you juggle, perhaps?' she enquired, in order to diffuse the predacious atmosphere. Stan didn't need to be asked twice. In delight, he leaped from the table. Picking up the set of silver sticks that the hostess immediately proffered him, he launched into an impromptu display of rhythmic chucking.

'That's pretty hot stuff,' commented Felicity as Stan threw the hollow baton between his legs. 'Do you practise much when you're alone?'

Stan was befuddled and slow. He felt like a character in someone else's plot and wished the writer would give him an annotated text so that he would know just how the story was supposed to come out and thus fix his position firmly within the overall scheme of things. In the absence of such guidance, all he wanted, just like water, was to float down the path of least resistance.

'I don't get much chance to practise,' he said, 'I've got no balls.'

The girls hooted with laughter, poured out yet more of the gallons of genuine Polish vodka they had smuggled back from a trip to Warsaw the previous year, and handed round the green, garlic-stuffed olives. Stan was mortified. He had committed social hara-kiri and knew full well that he had only himself to blame. Now all he wanted was to return to his own home, where he knew exactly what problems he might expect to encounter and could therefore thoroughly prepare to deal with them. He wanted to be appreciated but not if social acceptability came at as high a price as sexual humiliation. He wished he could leave. But this would be bad manners and he therefore knew that he would not.

Paul's mother, said Madeleine, was organising a society christening for her only granddaughter. Madeleine was less than unenthusiastic about this but could do nothing to prevent the occasion. If the dowager marrow, as they liked to call the market gardener's widow from the heart of Lincolnshire, wished to spend her fruit-gotten gains on impressing her deeply shallow and ultimately tedious friends, that was none of Madeleine's affair. She knew that if she felt strongly about the event then her destiny was in her own hands and it was up to her to call it off, but her husband wanted only the best for his daughter, explained the anxious parent, and the best for other people always came at a price to oneself.

'Very deep,' said Felicity, 'but my inner tubes are empty and my fuel tank needs filling, if you know what I mean.' Stan wondered how long she could keep it up. And then he wondered if she winked like that at all the boys, or if he should continue to take it personally. He didn't like Felicity. She wanted to draw him in as a satellite around her compelling, luminescent forcefield and knew that he would not dare refuse. Which did not mean, in the least, that he might fancy her. Because he didn't. It wasn't that sort of force at all.

Madeleine, the hostess with the mostest, returned to the room with a whole series of elaborately coloured dishes, none of which Stan recognised. He admired the opulence of the couple's gastronomic life but would never choose to spend his own hard-earned wages in its emulation. The food was good though.

'And what's this one?' he asked, poking at a piece of terracotta oven-to-tableware, knowing that to flatter the hostess's cooking skills would decrease his chances of again being asked to demonstrate his manual ones.

Eliza, who had said nothing for quite some time and did not seem to be enjoying her food, pointed out that Stan appeared to have a very poor short-term memory. It was the same Tuscan dish they had shared only a few days earlier at a bistro in Stoke Newington.

'Officer, I've never seen this dish before in my life,' he quipped. She must be confusing him with someone else, Scoop perhaps?

Eliza did not smile but pointed out that it was he who was mistaken. Stan, once again, felt that he was losing a battle in which he had not realised he was supposed to play a part. But he was not mystified by Eliza's sudden swings of mood, understanding as he did the special needs of woman and realising that she might well be suffering from the hormonal effects of premenstrual tension.

Felicity slammed down her cutlery and, smacking her lips loudly, got up to leave. She was off clubbing now with her new mate, Emily, she told them. She didn't want to be rude to her friends but neither did she feel like being middle-aged with them. Stan was glad when she skipped out of the door, looking, for all the world, like a million dollars and smothered in her pink, fluffy, fake-fur wrap. Girls like that spelt trouble.

But her presence was essential to the balance of the evening. She could be intensely annoying but you noticed her absence. 'Pudding without Felicity is like a life without love,' said Eliza.

'Good thing you're about to leave then, my middle-aged friend,' said Madeleine, 'because there isn't any.' Stan voluntarily moved to kiss her cheek. 'You are the hostess with the mostest,' he said, because it was true.

'I don't suppose I'll be seeing you again,' said Madeleine breezily, as she breathed him goodbye, oblivious now to his pock-marked features, 'but do remember, when you get home tonight and dream about Felicity, that it's nothing to worry about. It's a stage every man has to go through.'

Paul moved to chastise his wife for this frankness with a guest, to whom he had warmed after a fruitful conversation about the quality of refereeing in the rugby world cup. But Madeleine was already in another place, comforting an apparently flu-ridden Eliza who, by this stage, had her face burrowed in a saturated tissue.

Waiting in the doorway, the two men shrugged at one another in bemusement. Stan was at a loss. It was he who should be crying, not Eliza. But the wound was only one of injured pride, he knew, since Madeleine was wrong about Felicity, of course.

waiting for god

On the day after Jerry Joneth was elected honourable Member of Parliament for Wandsworth South-East, he bought his wife a dog.

'You'll be spending a lot of time by yourself at nights now,' he told her, 'since I feel it's my duty to the constituents who voted for me so loyally to take an active part in their representation in the seat of the oldest of world democracies.'

Rebecca thought he was a pompous ass, and in a finely felt appreciation of the donor's inner being decided to call her new pet 'God'.

God was wild. Each morning, when Jerry went off to do whatever it was that he did and about which his wife didn't choose to ask, Rebecca would take her shaggy beast on a long walk over the Heath, around the pond and up the hill. God was hairy and covered with mud and totally out of control. Whatever Rebecca might think about the rest of her husband, his taste in household pets was impeccable.

Then Rebecca had a moment of inspiration and she went out to a special shop in Covent Garden and bought a Chinese kite and a plastic, yellow Frisbee. While God darted from one part of the Heath to another in order to retrieve the flying disc, the woman who had been Mrs Joneth for as long as she could remember would raise the red and green dragon high above her head and control it by string from the ground as it soared away into the clouds. She knew it was pathetic but she'd never been so happy. God had changed her life.

One day, as she walked around the Heath in the long, flowing hippie skirt she had saved since her student days and which Jerry didn't like her to wear, but which had now become highly fashionable once again, she came across a group of youths sitting in a ring around a big, thick tree trunk. She recognised the type from her student days in hall and gazed at them in nostalgia. But God lived in the present. He smelled something cooking and that was that. Charging towards the ring of hand-holding youths at a cracking pace, he leaped over the chain of hands and right into the heart of the love circle. And then he looked back at Rebecca and barked. Alerted to her presence, the tree-huggers turned around and smiled.

'Hey, nice skirt,' called out a young lady with hennaed hair and a stud in her nose.

Rebecca, feeling unaccountably self-assured, sat down and joined the ring, while God frolicked happily, at one with the spirits of nature.

'Nice dog,' said the woman, patting his grey and matted hairs. 'What are you called, Bonzo?'

The young people laughed at the name and said that they

thought it was great. Rebecca was pleased with her choice and wanted to tell them how it had come about but, somehow, it was no longer relevant. The friendly woman told Rebecca that she lived for love in a van near the Elephant and Castle. The world's ecosystems were a mess, she said, and everyone had to take a stand.

Rebecca said she quite agreed. She herself had started sending postcards with pictures of torture victims on them to Chile on behalf of Amnesty International. The girl said she used to do that, too, and there were so many things to worry about, but she'd moved on to the ozone layer herself. It was all too gloomy, she said, shaking her head, but, in the meantime, did Rebecca fancy a puff?

Rebecca felt naughty. She looked around the ring of people. Most of the men had matted dreadlocks, remarkably like God's. Some of them were what Rebecca generally called 'coloured' and most of them wore khaki anoraks and brightly coloured denim jeans. One man, who was more darkly coloured than the rest, had a woolly bobble hat and purple reflective sunglasses even though it was a cold, sunless day. Rebecca thought he was terrific. She had always liked bright colours but had never known how to wear them. On being elected Jerry had offered to send her to a colorification stylist who would tell her whether she was an autumn or a winter girl, and Rebecca had said that it was kind of him to care but, personally, she would settle for a dog.

She asked the purple-bespectacled man if she could try his glasses on and he said, 'Hey, gladly, lady, for sure.' She realised it was a long time since she'd heard English spoken like that, and felt that she must be a hundred and six. But the naturals didn't seem to care. They made her feel welcome and she thought it was genuine. She knew that Jerry would murder her if he ever found out but, gleefully, she said yes to the offering and took a puff at the spliff when it was presented to her. She really wanted to wipe the end clean just for hygiene reasons but thought that this might not be considered good form so she just plopped the reefer in her mouth, closed her eyes and breathed in heavily.

Almost immediately she felt a burning sensation at the back of her throat and coughed and spluttered and thought she might choke. But nobody laughed at her and a man with a stud in his cheek and four silver rings in his ear clapped her vigorously on the back and said that the first burn was always the worst. 'Relax into it,' he told her, 'have another puff, enjoy.' God, taking a leaf out of his mistress's book, appeared to be relaxing already and began to snore loudly. Instead of passing the spliff straight on around the circle, Rebecca took another drag. She sensed that this was not the normal etiquette of drug-taking but also sensed that no one would mind. Then, quite suddenly, she felt as if her mind had been liberated from her body and was beginning to float high above the solid, rooted tree as it looked down on a woman in her thirties who had somehow lost her way.

'I've got lost,' she explained expansively to the group surrounding her, 'I don't know where I am.'

'Hey, lady,' said Purple Glasses, 'we're all lost out here. It's the way things are.'

Rebecca inhaled heavily for a third, lung-expanding time and then, regretfully, handed round the spliff to the left, and the hennaed girl took it from her and began to speak. Just like vintage port, thought Rebecca, as she watched the thin, white roll being passed hypnotically around the enchanted circle, always to the left, just like cigars at dinner and soda and lemonade and snowballs and sherry and vodka and traffic lights and fireworks and Catherine Wheels and Christmas crackers and candlesticks and shoe brushes and dog biscuits. Just like.

When she awoke, everyone had left. It was cold and windy and she felt a bit shamefaced and thought, perhaps, that she had dreamed the whole bizarre incident. But then she looked up in front of her and saw God, whose lead had been tied loosely around the tree. He was awake and alert and had been guarding her as she slept. She jumped up with a spring in her step and walked over to the trunk to hug her beloved companion. As she did, he turned towards her and barked and she saw that, on the top of his head, a pair of purple-reflective sunglasses were balanced like a strange, modern Alice band.

Rebecca untied God from the tree and let him run away from her, barking and leaping and throwing his long grey mane all over his tough, little body in the wind. In both hands, she grasped the glasses firmly and she headed for home.

x-rated movie

'*X-Rated Movie* is neither X-rated nor a movie. It is the name of a new multi-media show which has been devised and is currently being performed by two women new to the London entertainment scene, Felicity Flower and Emily Jackson. The action takes place in the roof space of the Battersea Arts Centre and the work itself is based around the women's already highly praised doubles' trapeze act. They refer to the piece as an example of T.T.E. which, to the uninitiated amongst us, stands for "total theatre experience" and, having been to the opening night yesterday, I can only agree with their definition of themselves.

'It goes without saying that this is, above all, a highly visual medium which demands to be seen and, over the radio, I could not begin to attempt to do justice to what I can only describe as a visual spectacle revolving around two physically compelling women, who play out an intimate partnership in mid-air, creating, at once, both an extremely intense performance and an atmosphere of such sexual tension that the audience is left breathless. The girls' sheer physicality is quite phenomenal. We watch helplessly as the two women leap around a set which consists solely of the two trapezes. Like the primates, which, as they intone repeatedly, we all are, they hang perilously from each other's nether regions, leaving the audience gasping in horrified concern. The dialogue, when intelligible, seems to deal with the perilous nature of dependency on other people, and is graphically highlighted by terrifying plunges from one extreme of the body to another.

'Much of the text is spoken upside down in mid-air. At one point in the show, Emily, who is a trained jazz singer, launches into a version of "Stormy Weather", rearranged especially for the show as part of a remarkable musical score composed by Emily's former piano accompanist, a rather stout young man called Bob Battle.

'The action itself, as far as it is comprehensible, is based around a young woman's journey towards self-fulfilment and is played out through the narration of her multifarious sexual relationships. But, as the two women intone, chant and contort twenty-five feet above a spellbound audience, the dialogue itself becomes part of a ritual demonstration of astonishing symbiosis. The artists are entirely dependent on one another, creating a bond of incredible intimacy and trust not only between the two of them but also with us, the audience, since, as spectators, we have to trust the two women not to fall as they perform their death-defying feats of flexibility and agility, hanging from each other toes, fingers and necks. It is,

Felicity, an astonishingly total theatre experience.'

'Well thank you very much, Pete, that's very kind of you. But only what we deserve of course.'

'Can I ask you, Emily, how it came about that you began to use trapeze as a medium in the first place and how much training you had to do to reach this level of skill?'

'Well may I say, Pete, I don't want to get this interview off to a bad start or anything but that is an incredibly stupid question. Of course the answer is that we had to train for a long time. You couldn't dream of doing a show like this otherwise. As Kurt, our former instructor and now an esteemed friend, so often reminds us, "trapeze is a serious medium for serious people". But, as we so often remind him, discipline itself is useless without pushing it an extra stage further. For us, particularly as women, trapeze is a tremendously powerful metaphor for life and strength and the meeting of challenges head on and we very much wanted to explore that aspect of its potential.'

'And may I congratulate you on what a fine job you've done with it, ladies. Can you tell me, Emily, how you actually went about the process of devising a piece that combines so many different media, and why, in particular, you chose to focus on the theme of sexuality?'

'Well, Pete, the thing is that we're both so multi-talented that we wanted to do a show in which we could show off our many combined skills. It's as simple as that really. And as for sexuality, well, sex is life, don't you think, Pete? And I think, we both think, that although this is a show about performance skills, in a world in which the easiest way for women to hang on to positions of power is by exploiting their physicality, then this is a visual way to highlight our essential femaleness. But we do realise that's a bit pretentious. Actually, what we really wanted was to just get out there in front of the public and wear saucy outfits. That's what the medium means to us. So what did you think, Pete, how did the outfits grab you?'

'Frankly, Emily, I was grabbed so hard that I think it might have affected my critical integrity but, Felicity, might I just ask you at this point about the fact that, as I understand it, before taking up trapeze as a full-time career, you used to be in charge of rubbish at Wandsworth Council? Is that correct, and, if so, have you brought anything out of your old life into your new one?'

'What extraordinary questions you ask! Of course I haven't. Nothing can come out of rubbish save more rubbish. The tedium of everyday existence can teach you nothing except a feeling of humility that you choose to participate. I was a very dissatisfied person, looking for a medium through which to express myself. I consider myself very lucky indeed to have met Emily who enabled me to achieve that aim. Most people aren't so fortunate. As soon as I could, I left rubbish behind me without any compunction.'

'Which brings me on to the question of mutual trust. How did you establish what is obviously such an intense symbiosis, Felicity?'

'Pete, mate, it's instinctual. Next question?'

'And Emily, how did you go about the actual process of creation?'

'Well, Pete, we just climbed up there onto the bars and said whatever came into our heads. The sentences that made us laugh the most became the text. Then we got my husband, Jack, to come and watch the rehearsals and whatever he laughed at we discarded.'

'But there is an element of self-deprecation in the whole show, isn't there? A fundamental ironic humour which deconstructs everything that you're trying to say?'

'We do like to have a laugh, me and Em, we like a good old chuckle.'

'And, finally, can you tell us why you chose to call the piece *X-Rated Movie*?'

'Because we wanted to make loads of money and we thought it was the quickest way to pull in the crowds.'

'As you heard earlier, Emily and Felicity arrived this week

at the Battersea Arts Centre near Clapham Junction. An unlikely venue, you might think, but yesterday was the opening night and Evelyn Burton went to see the show. Evelyn, as Emily says, there is a lot of humour in the piece, but it's ultimately brutal, also, don't you think?'

'Indeed. Very. The one thing that struck me last night was that the audience was afraid to laugh, which, quite frankly, may have a lot to do with the fact that we were all terrified that they would fall off and kill themselves. As the girls have said, the trapeze is an astonishingly forceful metaphor for life, setting up a very particular relationship between watcher and performer. I, for one, found it an incredibly powerful performance in both the literal and the metaphorical sense of the words. The girls' bodies are simply astonishing.'

'So can we take it that you enjoyed it, then? It was a theatrical evening in the best sense of the word.'

'Indeed. Very. But enjoyment isn't the right word. One admires it a great deal and one can laugh wryly at the tremendous wit and verve that the girls use to deconstruct themselves. But, on a purely emotional level, one can respond to the incredible strength that both girls demonstrate. I can, quite honestly, say that I've never seen anything quite like it. To be perfectly frank, as I said earlier, for most of the time I couldn't listen to the dialogue at all, and was simply anxiously hoping that I wasn't about to witness a fatal accident.'

'I do agree with you, Evelyn, that the quality of the trapeze work is stupendous and so different to anything we've seen before. Would it be too much to say that the discipline is finally coming into its own as an artform. How well was the theatrical integrated into the physical, do you think?'

'Indeed. Very. Again, I feel rather more generous in this regard than, as I understand it, do a lot of the critical community, although they all, may I say, very much enjoyed the visual nature of the show. My understanding of the somewhat limited plot was not assisted, may I add, by a major misprint in the programme synopsis, in which an "s" is, unfortunately, omitted so that "she" reads as "he", and because of which I thought that it was the Emily character's boyfriend who was in love with the Felicity character's father and not the Emily character herself. This confusion of gender, I have to say, totally distorted my sense of the narrative, and, I know it is a trivial point, but I would strongly advise the women to get this sorted out before they go on their British tour.'

'Evelyn, thank you very much for your comments and for that neat lead into the fact that *X-Rated Movie* continues at the Battersea Arts Centre until 24 May and then goes on to Guildford, Basingstoke and Glasgow.'

'Hey, Evelyn, they've gone now. Did you really enjoy the show?'

'I didn't understand a word of it, mate. But the tall, blonde one was something else entirely. She didn't leave her number in the studio by any chance, did she?'

yielding to weakness

Madeleine hated going to Islington. Susan lived there.

'You're being silly,' said Paul, 'you're being very silly indeed.'

Madeleine knew perfectly well that she was being silly. She had been married for some years now and had lived with Paul for even longer. As far as she was aware, her husband hadn't set eyes on Susan since a cricket match tea in 1989 but that was exactly why Madeleine thought it was all very suspicious, indeed. If Paul felt nothing for his ex-girlfriend, then why the hell did he get all touchy every time Madeleine mentioned her name?

Paul was exasperated but felt shamefully flattered. He wasn't remotely touchy, he told his, let's face it, absurdly jealous wife. Susan was simply no longer relevant to his universe. You go through phases in your life, he said, and then you move onto others. Susan belonged in a different phase and there was no place for her in this one. You had to cut out all of your previous lives at their roots, he said, as Madeleine began to look extremely grumpy, or the new ones would never have healthy soil from which to spring. She should consider the absence of Susan as a health issue.

'You see,' she claimed, triumphantly, 'that's exactly my point. What you're actually saying, and you can't possibly deny it, is that the very fact that Susan exists in this world at all has a meaning for you and, by implication, her presence in ours would be unhealthy.'

Paul gave up. This was all too contorted for him. 'Of course Susan has some significance for me,' he said, 'I bloody lived with her for four years. But now, for some obscure reason which at this point in time is very unclear to me, I live with you.'

Madeleine and Paul never argued. Well, very rarely, anyway. Both of them claimed to hate confrontation. But Paul was really losing patience with his infuriatingly contrary wife. Was Madeleine deliberately trying to annoy him?

'I don't know how to convince you,' he said, 'and I hope you're not going to get into this mood every time we come to Islington. I paid good money to join the Almeida mailing list and I intend to make full use of its facilities.' He went over to the bar and pre-ordered them both an interval glass of white, but not the house variety. The theatre was swarming with disarmingly cultured people so that the couple had to make a huge effort not to touch each other with any part of their impeccably turned-out bodies. Madeleine was perfectly well aware that she was being immensely irritating but to her way of thinking (a) the story just didn't make sense and (b) she was quite enjoying all the attention. Paul had lived with the superbly highly strung Susan for years and years and then, one day, he met Madeleine, fell in love and left Susan, just like that. He would try his best never to blight Susan's future by ever setting eyes on her again, he had said to her in a noble, slightly self-important sort of way, it was the best thing for both of them. Susan howled and threw a shoe at him, calling him a reprehensible bastard and a moral cop-out. Paul ducked and the shoe flew out of the window, landing squarely, seven floors below, on the shining bald pate of one of their more elderly neighbours.

But Paul's was a solemn vow to which he had faithfully adhered. Apart from the cricket club do, that is, which couldn't be avoided for career promotional reasons. Madeleine hadn't accompanied him to the event and Susan had arrived in a supportive posse made up of a large number of the couple's former mutual friends who now considered her ex-boyfriend a real cad and had cut him out of their lives completely. His pride had been piqued and his emotions hurt by this betrayal of old friendship and, all these years later, he had still felt himself unable to approach the group to say hello. When he went home and told Madeleine all about the encounter, his wife was not surprised. She found it impossible to credit that someone with whom you had spent most of your student years and with whom you had hitch-hiked all over the Far East, including the closed parts of North Korea – which was really something at that time – could no longer stir up deep-lying emotional whirlpools within you. It was hardly credible.

Paul returned from the bar with a pre-Ben Jonson gin and tonic. He could tell that his wife was still sulking. Well, okay, perhaps he shouldn't have thrown away the old butterdish without asking her but Pyrex is so old-fashioned and it was hardly worth making a fuss about a shabby piece of kitchenware. He stared at his volatile wife grimly and said, 'I can't believe you're really going to pursue this line of argument all evening. It's just ridiculous.'

Madeleine knew. But that wasn't the point. She wanted to be petulant. She had a right to be petulant. She was Paul's wife and she would be petulant, if she felt so inclined. All the way through the first act she scanned the audience continually. This was Susan's local theatre. It was eminently possible that Susan was right there in the auditorium, at this very second, just watching the two of them and staring. Madeleine might catch her eye at any moment or find herself in the queue behind Susan in the ladies' toilet. She wondered what they would say to each other and practised some imagined dialogue. It would be intolerable, quite intolerable. The first act had already finished by the time Madeleine realised that it had begun and, incidentally, it wasn't remotely funny. She didn't know why they called it a comedy. It was very tragic, in fact, and it made her come over all weepy. Paul passed her a handkerchief and wished she would pull herself together.

Two more hard-going acts later, as the pair located their pre-ordered interval Chablis, Madeleine still looked explosively depressed. Paul could bear the burden of her emotional ill-being no longer and, resignedly, conceded defeat. 'Look,' he said, 'all I want is for you to be happy and enjoy the play, okay? So I'm going to give you exactly what you want. I can quite honestly say that I was sitting all the way through the first half of that play thinking about Susan and how much she always enjoyed Ben Jonson and what pure comic enjoyment she got out of his plays. And then I turned round and I gazed at you, sitting there as miserable as sin, and blowing your snotty nose all over my hanky and I thought, fuck that, why the hell did I ever leave high-spirited, fun-loving Susan for this miserable, wretched old hag? What on earth could have possessed me? So, there you go. Happy now?'

Madeleine had known all along that she was right. But now that Paul had confirmed her worst fears she felt terrible. She said she had to call the babysitter straight away and rushed to the toilet where she sat on the seat and bawled her eyes out. Madeleine and Paul were seated on the far end of row D and, when she arrived back late for the second half, the other people had to get up to let her in, mumbling loudly about her antisociability. She didn't care. They were all laughing with their big bellies and finding the whole play riotously comic. How could they? Insensitive, callous, unfeeling bastards.

After the play, when they walked back to the Volvo, they saw that the front driver's window had been smashed and someone had stolen their brand-new *A to Z*.

'I don't like to say I told you so,' said Madeleine, with bad grace. Paul insisted that it was nothing to get upset about. Everything was under control. He had purchased fully comprehensive three-star insurance and the *A to Z* had been a complimentary bonus gift. They drove home in silence but it took ages because they got lost and, without the atlas, they could do nothing.

The next morning, as Madeleine sat at her desk, staring at a photo of her long-since-past wedding day, the telephone rang.

'Brian,' she shrieked with delight as the voice of her childhood sweetheart came booming down the line and she joyously recalled treasured moments from their shared but misspent youth. On leaving school, Brian had emigrated to Canada and broken her heart but they were seventeen at the time so it was easily reparable. They'd remained in frequent correspondence since that date and, in all these years, as Madeleine had kept in touch with his blossoming career as a tree surgeon Out West, and he with hers as a personal scent consultant to the glamorous wives of the famous, she had never once mentioned in the correspondence that she had in the interim got married and had a child.

They had a lot of catching up to do, that's for sure, they both exclaimed like schoolchildren waiting for first break. Madeleine and Brian wanted the meeting to be perfect, just like the old days. They'd go for a walk around Kensington Market, just like they used to, and stare lustfully at leather pilots' jackets and Chelsea boots. God, don't the decades fly by.

Madeleine's mother had always had a particular penchant for Brian, believing firmly that one's first love was always the strongest, and had given Madeleine's number to her daughter's first boyfriend without any need for persuasion. That Brian had been a gorgeous kid. Just gorgeous.

In turn, Madeleine, also, needed little persuasion. She took the afternoon off work willingly and, exactly like in the old days, they met up at Kensington High Street tube station by the ticket machines. Just like the old days, Brian hadn't bought a ticket and, just like the old days, Madeleine told him off for jumping the barrier. 'You know me, Mad,' said Brian, 'I've always been a bit of a rebel, a reckless frontiersman, if you like to put it that way. It's what drew you to me, as a girl, don't you remember? And, well, maybe, it's what still does?'

They reached out for each other's hands and looked into each other's eyes with a profound sense of nostalgia for innocence and lost romance and things that would never be the same again. They were both different people now, they whispered, unable to let go of each other's fingertips, and yet they were still both the same people at heart. They had grown layers of experience but this made them only more interesting, more rounded individuals. Brian spoke soft and low and said that he'd never thought of himself as a romantic guy but this, well, this was really something.

In McDonald's, for a bit of a laugh, Madeleine ordered a strawberry milkshake and sucked at it noisily through a thick plastic straw while Brian pursued a ginger beer.

'There's something I've got to tell you,' said Madeleine. 'It can't wait any longer.'

Feeling exceptionally manly, Brian put his finger to Madeleine's pouting lips and told her to hush. He didn't need to know, he said, he was only in England for a few days. It had been fantastic to see her and to spend some time with her and to speak to her but they both knew that to turn back the clocks was impossible. It was enough just to sit and hold hands and share an eat-in milkshake.

'Drink-in,' said Madeleine. 'I think you'll find you mean "drink-in". You can't eat a milkshake.'

Brian smiled and said that it was really amazing how people never change. Madeleine had always been a pedant. Stuff like that was so unimportant. He was surprised she hadn't learned such a simple lesson over all these years, and even more so now that she was married with a child.

Madeleine made a mental note to give her mother a really serious dressing-down for being a blabbermouth but Brian, once again, put his finger to her lips and sybillated a soft, sensual noise. In the past this gesture had caused Madeleine to melt away at the knees; in the present it was no different. She didn't ask Brian a thing. She didn't want to know. She was having a truly fabulous day and, as he said, it was best to leave it at that.

Slowly, they walked back to the tube, holding hands. In one smooth, elastic gesture, Brian hurdled majestically over the barrier, turned, blew Madeleine a poignant, farewell kiss, and then, silently, he disappeared into the bowels of the earth forever.

Madeleine went home to retrieve Sophie from the clutches of the babysitter and her young companion who worked at the local bakery. As she entered the living-room, the couple were interlocked violently on the sofa, eating Madeleine's special chocolates and watching an appallingly vicious video. It was the babysitter's first boyfriend. Madeleine sent them home early. She knew it would be nice while it lasted but they'd both move onto higher things. She decided not to tell Paul about her day out with Brian.

zero

Felicity particularly enjoyed a hands-on warm-up session. All of the participants were encouraged to throw themselves flamboyantly around the room in a whirlwind of untrammelled emotion. In her particular case, this process of letting go involved the exuberant hoisting of her skirt right up and over her head, thereby revealing a pair of remarkably unsoiled ivory silk French knickers.

Madeleine was embarrassed by this laissez-fairground behaviour. She did realise that the idea was to delve into some of those deep, dark emotions that lie latent within us all, but she did not feel that the exposure of her inner thighs could play an active part in this pursuit. Anyway, now that she had given birth and her stomach wasn't quite as flat as it once used to be, she was a little more restrained with her folds of flesh. She no longer felt sexy. Her doctor had assured her that the problem was psychosomatic and that, given time and an understanding husband, it would soon disappear. Meanwhile, she kept her quads to herself, and she hoped with all her heart that her little problem didn't give Paul an excuse to wander from the straight and narrow while she and Felicity and Eliza all took part in a self-expression drama workshop weekend.

Last year they did *Lear*, which had all been terribly highbrow, but now, with Felicity transformed into a minor cult icon and, altogether, a little too creatively arrogant for her own good, the professional performer among them had persuaded the other two to attend an active improvisation group session organised by a critic who had introduced himself to Felicity after giving a glowing review of her trapeze show on Radio Four.

Evelyn Burton considered himself to be a very gifted artiste. His many creative talents were wasted as a journalist on the Thursday Arts page. He should be out there, hands on the dials, controlling the moves, making it all happen. But money and other people held you back. And that was hard. Were he a novelist, for example, he could sit at home and be productive all by himself but in his heart he had recognised that his talents lay in an entirely different field – the direction of others. He had chosen a tough path to follow. Still, he was glad Felicity had turned up to be directed, even though she'd brought two friends along and one of them was married. He thought he could achieve some fine results with Felicity. She was, as she had told him expansively over the telephone, very open-minded about her creative expressiveness. As the group collectively limbered up to the minimalist sounds of a Finnish percussionist whom Evelyn much admired, the director appreciated his star participant's flowing form and, more even than that, her exemplary taste in silk underwear.

Felicity began to hug Eliza. Now that she was a professional performer, she could justifiably claim to be in touch with every part of her body. It was the kind of career she'd dreamed about her whole life and she particularly loved the way she could take off all her clothes in the name of high art and nobody would blink an eye. She only wished that her performance partner, Emily, could be there too so that they could both have a good laugh at the way Evelyn was drooling over her drawers. But he's an influential fellow, is what old-hand Emily had said, let him go ahead and drool. If he wants to slobber, just be there to wipe up the spittle.

Eliza responded warmly to Felicity's embrace. In just one year, her friend seemed to have discovered some new source of energy from within herself and then, miraculously, she had learned how to tap it. Eliza was gutted. Stan had also found a new source of energy. She was called Louise. It made Eliza so mad. Stan had demanded all of Eliza's attention for months. He had problems which he liked to air at great length while she listened dutifully, sighed and pulled meaningful, sympathetic expressions. And then, just as they were beginning to get somewhere, and maybe, she had thought, just maybe, they might even, one day, just perhaps, achieve the 'P' word – although, as Madeleine had pointed out very firmly, this was a very macho attitude to sex and penetration wasn't everything by any stretch of the imagination, with which Eliza entirely agreed, of course – but, anyway, just as she was getting somewhere close to persuading Stan that sex was not a cheapening and dirty experience and could, extraordinarily, be a pleasurable way to express one's affection for another person, this bloody Louise, apparently, rang up Stan and informed him that she'd made a terrible mistake and that Parvin, much as he was a wonderful person, was not the wonderful person for her. To Eliza's infinite chagrin, however, Stan was.

Stan had believed himself to be more sinned against than sinning. Eliza had believed herself to be more dignified than sympathetic. Fucking bastard, she had said to her friends, as they packed their weekend bags into the back of the rusted but nonetheless glamorous Spitfire that Felicity had bought with the profits from the video of her show, which was selling like hotcakes in W. H. Smith, mostly to chronologically challenged men who liked watching women in saucy outfits. Felicity had instructed Eliza that her problem was one of focus. Madeleine is looking for domestic comforts, said Felicity as the three of them piled into a car which was designed for only two. And Felicity's looking for self-fulfilment through creativity, said Madeleine, whose elbow was squashed against the window-screen wiper switch, which continually clicked on and off and on again as the car moved away from the kerb. But Eliza, they both agreed, more in sorrow than in anger, Eliza is looking for love.

Eliza grimaced and told them not to matronise her. She was distraught but she was perfectly okayish, if they knew what she meant.

'That Stan,' said Felicity, 'he was a waste of space. You can't love a man who's got no balls.' All three girls were by this stage intimately familiar with Stan's many sexual insecurities, to a degree which would have shrivelled his potential forever had he known. But, in the end, all the best advice in the world can't raise the dead. Louise from Hell had got what she deserved, considered Felicity who had chosen not to tell Eliza that Stan had rung her up on more than one occasion to ask her the name of a good gym or because he just happened to need some advice about his waste disposal. It was a pile of shit. Madeleine and Felicity had agreed that, in this instance, what you don't know can't hurt you. Eliza needed to put Stan firmly behind her, which was considerably more than she'd managed to do in his presence. They would all forget about idiot men and just enjoy the weekend away, they had agreed, packing the vodka. It would be just the three of them.

'Eliza is beautiful,' shouted out Felicity, as she took both hands off the wheel and stuck an Edith Piaf tape into the deck.

'Felicity is bloody reckless,' shouted out Eliza, as she

grabbed for the controls. And then they all began to shriek out a well-practised chorus in unison as their favourite theme tune blared out at the top end of the volume range.

'NI LE MAL, ÇA M'EST BIEN ÉGAL. C'EST PAYÉ, BALAYÉ, OUBLIÉ. JE ME FOUS DU PASSÉ.' La La La, sang the girls, who couldn't remember any of the lyrics but enjoyed making up fake French words as they went along.

Felicity may have been a performer but singing wasn't her medium. She didn't care. She was still happily warbling her tuneless anthem as the Spitfire steamrollered its clankety way into Wells High Street, which was really quite cute in an Olde English toffee fudge kind of way, decided the girls, but a dead loss on the Olde Polish alcohol front. This was a shame, they agreed, since they could all do with a quick one before entering the House of Burton, a dynasty founded, according to Felicity's prolific sources, from the vast sums of money that Evelyn's father had made out of fireproof sofas, a market whose potential he had exploded when it first came to public consciousness in the early seventies.

Evelyn rushed to open the vast, wooden door and then led the three girls into a large gothic hall, where a wide variety of other participants were already sporting their casual gear and limbering up to the hypnotic rhythms of Philip Glass.

'Just join in when you feel like it,' said Evelyn, 'introduce yourselves, don't be shy, make yourselves at home.'

'Curious, is it not?' pointed out an ascerbic Madeleine, 'that all of the other participants are women.' Already engaged in the getting off of her kit, Felicity, the consummate professional, assured her friend that this was perfectly normal for this kind of workshop. Eliza was disappointed. She had hoped for the appearance of Mr Miracle, someone who, unlike Stan, might rise to a challenge.

And then Felicity, without the slightest trace of self-consciousness, threw her skirt high into the air and displayed her camiknickers lovingly to the world. Evelyn adored the spectacle. He worshipped at Felicity's thespian limbs and begged her to lead the group, introducing her as 'very well known if you're in the business'. The other women, who were all chattering happily and hoping to achieve catharsis, were impressed by the introduction and knew that they ought to appreciate Felicity if they wanted Evelyn to appreciate them, which, naturally, they did.

Felicity immediately assumed control. She had never imagined it would be otherwise. She explained to the group that they were going to work on conceptualisation. You are all sources of energy, she said, and now you are going to act out those sources. The women were selfconscious and stood around in their shell-suits looking a bit foolish and wondering how to begin. Evelyn sat on a chair, drinking a mug of coffee and soaking in the atmosphere. Felicity outshone everyone in the room. She radiated energy. More accurately still, she was energy. Despite his professional aspirations, Evelyn wished everyone else in the room would go home instantaneously so that he could fuck Felicity senseless in the Grand Hall of his fireproof childhood. Felicity was unaware of his existence. She was in the throes of performance.

'I am petrol,' she said, 'volatile, powerful, smooth, sexy, flowing, combustible. And this is how I am.' Quite out of the blue, she suddenly threw herself at Evelyn, who had fortunately put down his mug, and, grabbing at his hands, she leaped up and thrust herself high onto his left shoulder from where she balanced on her hip bone, her hands in his, her arms stretched out wide, looking for all the world like Superwoman in mid-flight.

All the anonymous women were anxiously hoping that they weren't expected to do anything quite so demonstrative but Madeleine and Eliza had grasped the notion and they, too, were up and running.

'I am wind,' said Madeleine, making turbulent, whooshing noises and throwing her body into the air in an ungainly, limbless sort of way.

'And I am spaghetti,' said Eliza, spinning round and round

in circles, throwing herself at the wall and then falling back onto the floor and collapsing into fits of giggles. 'I am not quite *al dente*.'

Evelyn regarded the workshop as his baby and he now watched it developing its own identity. He considered this growth process meant that he could sit on the side and do nothing, since the best way to learn was through self-discovery. He was a natural at teaching.

A large lady in pink towelling began to get excited and told the group that she was a train shooting through the tunnel of love. An even larger lady called Samantha, wearing what might well have been material stripped from the top of a snooker table, suddenly shrieked out the word 'Eureka' and told the group that she was imagination. Felicity said that was great, really conceptual. Samantha was thrilled and began to feel a little more confident. 'Eureka, Eureka,' she shrilled, storming around the room like a bumper car on acid. But she was much larger than a bumper car and it was hard to avoid her. Evelyn made mental notes. He still wanted to fuck Felicity badly but was now considering the possibility of making a bit of extra money on the side by writing a story about self-fulfilment for the outsized. Cruel but with a high human interest value. It would be okay; his editor was very slim.

Many fun-filled hours later Evelyn was still mulling over the craftsmanship of his perfect opening sentence as he showed the house guests where they would sleep. Most of the women had come up from the town for the day and their husbands had arrived at the end of the workshop to ferry them back to Wells. Eliza and Madeleine were not surprised to discover that they would be sharing a twin room whilst Felicity had been allocated a double to herself at the other end of the corridor.

'What a joker the guy is,' they said but Felicity didn't care. She might lock the door or she might not. She hadn't yet decided. She made her own decisions, now, and was unflustered by the burden of choice. It was an extraordinarily empowering sensation. While Evelyn went to work on some ideas, the three women walked down to the town. They found Samantha waiting for them in the only local pub of ill repute and proceeded to get totally smashed whilst a delighted Samantha ran around the pub like a puppy, yelping out loudly that she was relativity. Many shots of straight vodka later, the women stumbled a raucous and highly inflammable path back to the House of Burton and toppled their way into their respective beds. This was so much more fun than they had ever had with *Lear* in Kingston. They could hardly credit the fortuitousness of Evelyn's crush on Felicity. Thank God for men.

Evelyn heard them come in. He had been waiting. He was wearing his brand-new black silk Calvin Klein pyjama bottoms, and no top. He was a man of action. Felicity had made him feel, once again, alive and young and full of critical faculties. She was a power socket and he was a plug. It was an extraordinarily empowering sensation. He waited for the noises of the night to cease and then, quietly but assuredly, he crept his way down the antique corridor of his boyhood years. He knew that Felicity had sensed the waves of energy flowing between them. He was confident that her door would not be locked. And, turning the wrought-iron handle, he realised that he was right.

It was very dark in the room. The four-poster bed loomed out from the middle-aged shadows. He peered into the obscurity of sexual desire and, silhouetted in the shadows of the night, he could not remember ever having seen anything more desirable than the curved and angular elbow of Felicity. Ludicrously, he tiptoed over to her marble form and then, almost unable to breathe, he bent down to kiss the joint at the far edge of her body. Her face was buried in the duck-down pillow but he knew that this was a fixed rule of the game. She could not be asleep when she felt the pure force of his presence in the room. It was quite impossible.

He skirted around the edge of the bed and then, panting silently, he clambered in, at long last clasping his ultimately cherished ambition to his heaving bosom. He closed his eyes and, as his love object slowly ran through the pretence of awakening in his arms and began to cling, lovingly, to the nape of his goose-like neck, Evelyn surrendered himself to his overriding passion. Which was a bit disappointing for her, really, since she had expected a much higher calibre performance.

'Bloody men,' she said to the others in the Spitfire on the way home the next day. 'Bloody typical, I couldn't believe it, all talk and no action. That's what it all comes down to in the end. Frustrating pigdogs.'

Madeleine and Felicity agreed entirely. But the exercise they had contrived on Eliza's behalf had been highly profitable, since the quickest way to erase someone from your universe is to replace that person with someone new.

'But it's by no means the best,' pointed out Felicity, as she stuck Edith's anthem back into the machine.

Very true, thought Madeleine, who had chosen not to tell her friends about an emotive day out she had spent recently with her childhood sweetheart, Brian. She had known she was right to bid him goodbye forever, but you couldn't explain that rationale to your heart or to your bits. Doctor Beavis had said it was only psychosomatic, of course, and he'd given her some really powerful lubrication, which was sure to do the trick. And Paul was a very understanding husband.

Eliza looked at her friends, immersed in their own worlds as they sang loudly and out of tune. They would soon be back in Wandsworth. Weekends were fine, especially when you achieved the 'P' word, and she didn't regret the time thrown away on Stan, she thought appositely, as she joined in the final, rousing chorus of Edith's well-known anthem. Oh no, she belted out loudly, she didn't regret a thing. But, as she faced the Junction 15/4B interchange for the second time in the past few months, Eliza screamed out the last line of the lyric and felt a tinge of weakening anxiety coursing through her. She knew it was pathetic and retrogressive and it troubled her immensely that the thought had even crossed her mind, but the immense and overwhelming prospect of starting all over again with someone new was wearying in itself. She'd been there and back this year with Gus and Jerry and Stan, and now, because it was Sunday evening and this was the M4 and tomorrow would be Monday, she knew that she would just get up in the morning, brush her teeth and start again from zero.